A DEADLY EMBRACE

Once on the ground, Bidai walked confidently into the jungle with Joe and Frank behind him. They were quiet as they moved through the tunnel-like pathway, again alert to the potential for ambush.

Ahead of them, Bidai slipped easily through the passage, without even rustling the leaves. Joe had just ducked under a low branch and was hurrying to keep Bidai in sight when he heard a muffled shout.

He turned and saw the branch shaking violently. A huge python hung from the limb, its brown and black spots undulating like trembling leaves. It was coiled around something, its body still moving into position to crush its prey. As the coils parted for a moment, Joe could make out Frank's face, twisted in agony. . . .

Books in THE HARDY BOYS CASEFILES™ Series

Available from ARCHWAY Paperbacks

THE HARDY BOYS

CASEFILES™

NO. 105

LAW OF THE JUNGLE

FRANKLIN W. DIXON

AN ARCHWAY PAPERBACK
Published by POCKET BOOKS

New York London Toronto Sydney Tokyo Singapore

AN ARCHWAY PAPERBACK *Original*

An Archway Paperback published by
POCKET BOOKS, a division of Simon & Schuster Inc.
1230 Avenue of the Americas, New York, NY 10020

Copyright © 1995 by Simon & Schuster Inc.
Produced by Mega-Books, Inc.

ISBN: 0-671-50428-2

First Archway Paperback printing November 1995

10 9 8 7 6 5 4 3 2 1

THE HARDY BOYS, AN ARCHWAY PAPERBACK
and colophon are registered trademarks of Simon & Schuster Inc.

THE HARDY BOYS CASEFILES is a trademark
of Simon & Schuster Inc.

Cover photograph from "The Hardy Boys" series © 1995
Nelvana Limited/Marathon Productions S.A. All Rights Reserved.

Printed in the U.S.A.

IL 6+

LAW OF THE JUNGLE

Chapter

1

"LOOK OUT!" Joe Hardy yelled.

Joe's stocky friend, Chet Morton, was standing on the other side of a long, narrow table set up in their social studies class at Bayport High. The table was covered with foods and objects from Pakistan. It had been set up for a report by Marsha Bailey.

Chet was trying to sneak his third Pakistani meatball, called a shami kebab, from the very end of the table. He was concentrating so hard that he failed to notice Biff Hooper, the home run champ of Bayport's baseball team, move in beside him.

When Chet turned with his meatball, he slammed into Biff. Chet rebounded off him and hit the table with a jolt. The objects seemed to jump into the air in a single motion. Most landed back on the still shaking table, but one ceramic replica of a Pakistani temple started to fly off the table several feet from where Joe stood.

"No," Marsha Bailey shrieked as she watched the miniature temple start its descent to the floor.

Joe threw his six-foot frame toward the temple, his blue eyes glued to it. He scooped the statue out of the air, pulled it to his chest with his left hand, and cushioned his fall with his right. Then he stood up with it still cradled in his arm as his classmates cheered.

"Nice catch," Chet said. "I would have been in big trouble if that thing had broken."

Marsha hurried over to examine the temple.

"It's still perfect!" she exclaimed, giving Joe a quick smile. "Thanks." He started to say she was welcome, but the bell rang before he got out the words.

As his classmates filed out of the room, they slapped Joe on the back. He smiled and joked with them but couldn't shake the worry that had been niggling at him all day, especially as he'd watched Marsha give her presentation.

Joe's report on Borneo was due in ten days, and he had barely started the research. He had thought the report on the world's third largest island would be a piece of cake since his dad, a well-known private investigator, was on assignment there. Fenton Hardy had agreed to bring back objects and information. Fenton was a week overdue, though, and Joe's report, which would make up eighty percent of his grade for the class, seemed to be in danger. Joe had also begun to worry if his dad might be in danger.

At his locker on his way out of school, Joe met up with his brother, Frank. "You're worrying about Dad again, aren't you?" Frank asked.

"Nah, Dad's okay. He can take care of himself," Joe lied.

He didn't fool his older brother, though. Slightly taller than Joe, with brown hair and eyes, Frank looked nothing like Joe. But the two boys thought alike.

"I'm worried about him, too," Frank said, frowning. "But it's probably just taking longer to clean up the details of the case."

Frank and Joe had just pushed out through the front door when they saw a bright yellow van parked at the curb. It was painted with cartoon characters holding packages and rushing around.

" 'Hey, it's Crazy Jay,' " Frank said. The line was actually from a Crazy Jay courier service radio spot, and Frank said it as an announcer would.

Crazy Jay was Jay Torres, who had graduated from Bayport High two years earlier and started his own courier service. He then landed the local franchise for an international overnight delivery service called Speed-A-Way.

"I wonder what he's doing here," Joe said as Jay stepped out of the van.

Wearing blue jeans and a Bayport baseball jersey, he was headed straight for Joe and Frank.

"You two must be on another case." Jay smiled slyly and waved a large manila envelope in the air. "It's marked Urgent."

"Thanks, Jay, but we're not on a case right now," Frank said as he took the envelope and turned it over. A form on the outside said the envelope had been given to Speed-A-Way in London. It was addressed to Frank and Joe at their home.

"Who do we know in London?" Joe asked, looking over Frank's shoulder.

"Beats me," Frank said as he ripped into the envelope.

Inside was a piece of folded paper, yellow and fragile with age. Frank opened it gently to reveal the outline of a large island covered with mountains, streams, and dots for towns. In one corner of the paper was a small section of the map drawn in even more detail. Both this section and the large map had two small *x*'s drawn on them not far from a river named Rajang.

"It's Borneo," Joe said. "I recognize it from my research. But what does it mean?"

Frank was unfolding a small piece of white paper clipped to the corner of the map. On it was a handwritten note: "Sending this with a British tourist. Guard it with your life. F.H."

Even without the initials, the brothers would have recognized Fenton Hardy's writing. They exchanged worried looks. Then Frank quickly refolded the paper and pushed it back into the envelope.

"Thanks, Jay," Frank said lightly.

"No problem," Jay threw back over his shoulder as he jogged to his van. "Good luck with your case."

Frank raised his eyebrows and frowned.

"Do you think he's right?" Joe asked. "Do we have a case?"

"I'm not sure," Frank answered. "But from that message, I'd say Dad is into something big. Let's hope we hear from him again soon. But right now we have to get to football practice or we'll have to do ten extra laps."

Practice seemed to last forever for Frank. No matter how he tried, he couldn't keep his mind on anything but the map that was tucked in a money belt under his sweatpants. It was Friday, and the team had no game scheduled for that weekend. Obviously the coach wanted to work them hard before letting them go for two days without practice.

When the guys finally broke, they hurried to get home. As Joe drove their van through Bayport, they tried to recall what they knew about the case their father was on. They remembered he'd been hired by a large pharmaceuticals firm.

"We've got to figure out the time difference between here and Borneo so we'll know when

Dad could call," Frank said as they neared their house.

"It's thirteen hours," Joe said without hesitation. "I know that much from my social studies report."

Frank glanced at his watch. It was six-thirty. "That means it's seven-thirty in the morning in Borneo," he said. "Dad's probably just finishing breakfast."

"Right, so he could call anytime," Joe added as he parked the van.

Fenton had last called a week earlier saying he was leaving his hotel in Sibu and heading into the jungle. He'd promised to call again from the town of Kijang, but so far they'd heard nothing.

"Let's keep this to ourselves until we hear from Dad," Frank said as he got out of the van. "There's no sense worrying Mom and Aunt Gertrude."

Joe agreed. They strolled into the house and talked about school and football practice during dinner. After clearing the table, they went upstairs and sprawled out in Joe's room, waiting for the phone to ring while they tried to do homework.

"Homework on a Friday night?" Laura Fenton said skeptically when she passed the room two hours later on her way to bed. "You're up to something. I can tell."

"He's got to call," Joe whispered as soon as

she had left. "If he doesn't, we have nothing to go on except that map."

By midnight both boys had gone to bed.

Frank awoke a short time later to the touch of Joe's hand on his arm. He sat up quickly and noticed that the digital clock by his bed said 3:00 A.M.

Joe held a finger to his lips. Then Frank heard it, the low rumble of a file cabinet drawer being rolled open. He was on his feet in an instant. Both guys sneaked carefully down the stairs toward their father's office.

The light was on in the small room, and now there could be no mistake. Someone was in there.

Joe stuck his head in the office door and saw two masked men rifling through their father's things. The taller of the two men spotted Joe and grunted a warning to his partner. Joe stepped into the room, planning to tackle the closer of the two. Before he could move, though, the man had grabbed a replica of an Aztec pyramid from Fenton's desk and fired it across the room. Joe ducked and the metal paperweight whizzed past his head, slamming into the wall behind him. The intruders dashed for the window.

Frank peered into the room before entering and just saw the taller burglar dive through the window. The second thief was about to leap outside when Frank hurled his body through the doorway and across the room. He caught the ankle of the shorter man, but the thief reached back and slammed his fist up and into Frank's chin. Frank lost his grip and fell to the floor as the thief slipped out the window.

Joe dove after him, doing a neat roll onto the lawn and landing on his feet. But the thieves had already disappeared into the night.

"I lost them," Joe complained when he'd hoisted himself back in through the office window.

"Yeah, but now we know we have a case," Frank offered. He was holding a file folder labeled Phillips Pharmaceuticals.

"I found this on the floor and, look, it's empty," Frank said, shaking the file folder upside down before handing it to Joe. "What do you want to bet those guys stole the contents?"

"So those guys may have been looking for information on Dad's case?"

"Could be," Frank said. "But why?"

Joe shrugged. Just then the phone rang and both guys jumped. "Dad!" they said in unison.

Joe picked up the receiver, but instead of his father he heard a woman with a foreign accent asking, "Is this the Hardy residence?"

"Yes," Joe said. "Who is this?"

"Dr. Michiko Tokunaga," the woman said. "I'm calling from the city of Kijang on the island of Borneo with news about Fenton Hardy."

"Is there a message from him?" Joe demanded. He was standing by the desk and felt his muscles tense as he waited for a reply.

"No," Dr. Tokunaga said. There was a moment of hesitation before she continued. "Fenton Hardy is too ill to send a message. I'm afraid he may be dying."

Chapter

2

JOE SANK into Fenton's chair, his mind reeling. He couldn't believe that his dad might be dying.

"Can you come to Borneo?" Dr. Tokunaga's voice demanded. Joe realized it was the second time she had asked the question.

"Yes, yes, of course we can," Joe stammered. "But what's wrong? What do you mean he's dying?"

There was a pause at the other end of the line followed by Dr. Tokunaga's slow, soft words. "I don't know. But we're doing all we can."

"Was there an accident?" Joe pressed.

Frank was across the desk from him, frowning.

"No," Dr. Tokunaga said. "It's an illness, though I don't know exactly what. All our tests . . ." Her voice trailed off. "He wandered into the hospital two days ago, desperately ill, then gave me your number, but told me not to call unless it became a true emergency. I'm afraid it is. This afternoon Mr. Hardy's fever shot up, his pulse is racing, and I don't know how much longer he can last."

"But there must be something you can do," Joe pleaded. Half a world away from his father, he felt utterly helpless.

"We're doing our best," Dr. Tokunaga insisted. "When can you get here?"

"I don't know," Joe replied. "But we'll leave as soon as we can."

"Come to the hospital at Kijang," Dr. Tokunaga said, "and hurry."

Joe hung up the phone slowly. "Dad's sick," he told Frank. "The doctor says we need to come to Borneo fast—because he may be dying."

"Did you talk to him?" Frank asked after a moment. "Are you sure this isn't somebody's idea of a joke?"

"I don't think so," Joe said, shaking his head. "The connection was bad—not like a local call. And I didn't recognize the voice."

Frank began to pace. "What's going on?" he asked seriously. "Dad goes to Borneo on a job for a pharmaceuticals company, then we get an old map that we don't understand, burglars break into Dad's office and steal a file about the case, and now this."

"Dad's sick, not hurt," Joe reminded his

brother. "How could that be related to the map or the burglars?"

"I don't know," Frank said, reaching for his father's phone directory. "But I think we'd better get to Borneo fast."

Forty minutes later, Frank had booked their flights and they were in their rooms packing. Just before dawn they woke Laura Hardy to explain their mission.

They had to talk their mother out of going with them, explaining that someone had to stay at home in case Frank and Joe got into trouble. They added that they'd call her to come if things were desperate.

Mrs. Hardy finally agreed to call the school on Monday morning and explain their absence. She also promised to try not to worry while she waited for news.

A couple of hours later Frank and Joe found themselves in the rear of a jumbo jetliner. The cramped quarters, combined with their restlessness, made for a long, nerve-racking trip.

Joe was barely able to focus on a book about Borneo he'd checked out from the library for his report. By the time they got across the Pacific Ocean, he was at least familiar with the geography of the island, which, he learned, was only slightly larger than Texas.

He had located the city of Kijang, along the Rajang River, in a region of central Borneo that was officially part of the country of Malaysia. He had also compared his modern map of the island to the hand-drawn map they had gotten from Crazy Jay's courier. The two x's on the map were about fifty miles up the Rajang River from Kijang.

Frank had brought along a paperback mystery, but he was too worried to read it. The book sat unopened on his lap while he stared out the window, watching the emptiness of the ocean below and thinking about his dad.

When they deplaned at the tiny Kijang airport, a blast of hot, steamy air hit them.

"Who turned on the furnace?" Frank exclaimed as they stepped onto the hard dirt surface in front of the small airport terminal.

They had been on airplanes of one type or another for more than twenty-four hours, traveling from Bayport to London to Singapore. From there they'd taken a small plane across the South China Sea to Kijang.

Now it was dusk on Sunday evening, but the temperature was still ninety-eight degrees, and the humidity was at least eighty percent—making both brothers immediately break into a sweat.

"I think I could collapse right here," Joe said.

"Maybe it will get better when the sun goes down," Frank suggested as they took their bags from a small cart that had been wheeled out to the plane.

They followed the half-dozen other passengers

through the doors of the terminal. It was only slightly cooler inside.

After a quick check through customs, they pushed through a second set of swinging doors to a dirt street.

"Hey, wait," Joe yelled, waving his hands.

Frank looked up to see a middle-aged man and women slide into the backseat of a battered brown car as a smiling driver swung their luggage into the trunk and slammed it shut.

"That's the last taxi," Joe said. "We have to get him to take us, too."

Joe and Frank lifted their bags and hurried clumsily toward the battered car, only to have the driver wave to them and slam his door. He made a tight U-turn and sped away, dusting Frank and Joe with dirt.

"Great," Joe said as he dropped his bag on the shoulder of the road. "We don't even know where the hospital is or if Dad is still . . ."

He left the sentence unfinished. Neither of the Hardys wanted to think their dad might already be dead.

They were both staring helplessly at the stretch of dusty road when a mud-caked green vehicle bounced up to them and stopped. The aging car had once been a compact sedan but had had its roof cut off so that it was open like a convertible.

The vehicle screeched to a halt, and dust billowed around it. A small, muscular, dark-skinned teenager vaulted over the door.

"Frank and Joe Hardy?" he asked with a thick accent, holding out his hand in welcome.

For a moment neither brother moved. Then Frank extended his hand and nodded.

"I'm Bidai," the stranger said with a smile. "Get in."

Joe was immediately suspicious. "How did you find us? No one knew what plane we'd be on."

Bidai smiled patiently and shook his head, as though ready to scold the guys, then spoke in halting but accurate English. "There are only two planes to Kijang today. You were not on the first, so the doctor hoped you would be on this one."

Frank and Joe exchanged looks.

"Doctor?" Frank said questioningly. He still didn't fully trust the stranger.

"Dr. Tokunaga," Bidai said, slightly irritated. "She says you need to come to the hospital quick. Your father is very ill."

Bidai opened the back door of the car and motioned for the guys to get in.

Instead, Frank pressed him. "You live around here?"

Bidai looked quizzically at Frank, but kept smiling. "I have lived here all my life," he said patiently. "My tribe has a longhouse outside of town."

"What tribe is that?" Joe asked casually.

"Iban," Bidai said, his chest swelling slightly

15

with pride. "We are great warriors." Again motioning for the guys to get in the car, he added, "And also very good drivers."

"I think we've found our ride," Joe said, tossing his bags into the crop-topped car and sliding into the backseat on the driver's side. Frank smiled grimly and walked around the car, tossing his bags into the front seat, and then climbing in beside Joe.

Soon they were careening down the street with Bidai at the wheel, easily outrunning their own dust cloud.

"Doesn't this town have any speed limits?" Frank asked, leaning over and yelling in Joe's ear.

"I don't know, but this guy is driving like a maniac," Joe yelled back.

The sun had completely disappeared over the horizon, and the sky grew increasingly dark as the car bounced down the dirt road. The jungle loomed menacingly on both sides of them, and Frank and Joe were relieved finally to see lights up ahead.

As they entered the outskirts of Kijang, they saw traditional houses, their floors set several feet above the ground on tall poles.

"Why are the houses on stilts?" Frank asked, leaning forward to yell in their driver's ear.

"Floods," Bidai yelled back over his shoulder. "It's dry now, but when the rains come, the Rajang River will run right through here."

Frank leaned back and watched the scenery change. As they climbed uphill, the dirt street gave way to cobblestone, and the bamboo houses were replaced by small, unpainted wooden ones.

Just then Bidai made a hair-raisingly fast left turn into a narrow alley.

"Do you know where you're going?" Joe demanded, holding on to the door to keep from sliding across the seat.

Bidai looked over his shoulder at the Hardys. Both brothers hoped he wouldn't crash.

"Short cut to the hospital," Bidai said casually, his foot still plastered to the floor.

"Look out!" Joe yelled, pointing ahead of them.

Bidai turned back around just in time to screech to a halt in front of three men and a rickety pushcart completely blocking the street.

Joe and Frank were nearly thrown into the front seat as the brakes squealed and locked. The guys looked up to see the three men lower themselves into crouched positions, as though ready to jump out of the way. But there was no fear on their faces—nor surprise.

The man with the cart suddenly thrust it violently away. As it clattered across the cobblestones, he reached across his chest and drew something small and silvery from his belt. It was a gun, and it was pointed straight at the car.

Chapter

3

"Don't move!" the gunman shouted. The man was short and dark. In the gathering gloom Joe's first impression was that he looked enough like Bidai to be the young Iban's brother.

Frank, Joe, and Bidai froze, and the gunman relaxed a bit, turning his head and using the pistol to motion his two buddies toward the car.

Joe was already in action, though. After vaulting out of the car, he hit the cobblestone street running. Before the gunman had time to aim, Joe was on him and knocking the pistol from his hand with a lightning quick karate kick. He followed this up with a hard right to the gunman's jaw. The pistol skittered into the shadows.

Frank meanwhile made a flying leap at the thug on the gunman's left. He landed in front of

18

the man and sank his left fist deep in his gut, then aimed a right uppercut to the chin as his opponent doubled over.

The man jerked his head to the side, and Frank's right barely grazed him. The man continued his sideways maneuver and kicked out expertly at Frank's midsection. Frank tried to give with the blow, letting himself roll backward.

From the corner of his eye, Joe saw his brother go down. Joe's opponent was staggering, so Joe sent him to the cobblestones with a last left hook, then turned to help Frank. As he did, he saw the third hijacker head for the car where Bidai still sat, watching the fight with his hands on the wheel.

"Stop him!" Joe yelled as the hijacker reached into the car and grabbed his and Frank's bags.

Bidai stood up and raised his hands helplessly as the thief took off with one bag in each hand.

Joe went after him, and even though the thief had a head start, the weight of the bags slowed him down. Joe made a flying tackle that sent both him and his quarry crashing to the ground.

In the scramble that followed, Joe managed to get one hand on his bag and sink his left knee hard into the thief's gut. There was a loud *oof* as the man recoiled, rolling away from Joe. Then he scrambled to his feet and fled empty-handed.

Joe picked up the bags and headed back to the car at a jog. He could see Frank coming toward him. The other two attackers had also disappeared into the night.

"What was that all about?" Frank asked as the two met in the shadows behind the car.

"Thieves," Joe said, shaking his head. "They seemed to want our luggage, and from the looks of the leader, they could easily be from the same tribe as our driver."

"I think we need to get some answers from Bidai," Frank said tensely. "He certainly wasn't any help fighting off those guys."

The two walked back to the car, and Joe swung the bags into the backseat. Bidai was busy moving the overturned cart out of the way.

"Some of your friends?" Frank demanded, walking up behind him.

Bidai turned. His eyes narrowed as he sucked in a long breath and pushed his chest out. "Are you accusing me?" he asked in a low voice.

"Well, you sure weren't any help," Joe said. "And why did you bring us down this alley anyway?"

"I told you it's a shortcut to the hospital," Bidai said, his hands balling into fists. "And I didn't know those men. They're thieves—you should let the police handle them."

"Yeah, but you could have helped us protect our luggage," Joe said.

"I can't believe there is anything in your suitcases worth risking your lives for," Bidai said.

"Your father needs you. You should be going to him now and not arguing like this."

Frank and Joe backed down. Bidai was right, though it would have been a different story if the map had been in the suitcases. As it was, the map was safely tucked inside Frank's money belt. Even though they didn't trust Bidai, they did need to get to the hospital fast. As they climbed back into the car, they only hoped that Bidai would get them there without any more trouble.

But the Hardys' worries only increased when Bidai brought the car to a bouncing stop in a patch of dirt that served as the hospital's parking lot.

"Four cars," Bidai said, glancing around the lot. "It must be a busy day."

The hospital itself was a white single-story building with peeling paint and a red tile roof. A row of small windows ran the length of it.

"First thing we've got to do is get Dad out of here," Joe whispered as they followed Bidai to the front door.

"I'm with you on that," Frank said. "He needs to be in a real hospital."

The single wooden door creaked when Bidai opened it, but as Frank and Joe entered the small building, a blast of cool air hit them.

"At least it's air-conditioned," Joe said.

"And clean," his brother added as they stepped onto the polished hardwood floor.

The walls were white and had been freshly

21

painted. There was no reception area, only a long hallway, with doors opening off both sides of it, giving way to small rooms.

"We'll find the doctor," Bidai said. "She'll help you, but watch out. She makes those thieves look nice."

Frank opened his mouth to ask Bidai what he meant, but before he could get the words out, a tall, blond man wearing a white lab coat stepped out of one of the doors. He was frowning intently and didn't seem to notice them as he closed the door and started walking quickly away.

"Wait," Frank called, starting after him.

The man's frown deepened as he glanced back over his shoulder at them.

"We're here to see Fenton Hardy," Joe said.

The man stopped dead in his tracks, turned, and eyed the boys curiously.

"And you are?" he asked, raising his eyebrows.

"Frank Hardy," Frank said, holding out his hand. "And this is my brother, Joe."

The tall man's frown instantly melted and was replaced with a warm, comforting smile.

"You've traveled a long way," he said.

"Yes, and we're anxious to see our father," Joe said. "Is the doctor here?"

"Of course, come with me," the man said. "I'm Dr. Tokunaga's assistant, Thomas Wilson."

The man's strange accent puzzled Frank. He couldn't quite place it but said nothing.

"How was your trip?" the now friendly Wilson

asked as he led them down the hall. "No problems, I hope?"

He opened a door marked Quarantine and seemed to be concentrating on Frank and Joe's faces as they walked toward the open door. Bidai followed.

"Nothing much," Frank said a bit sarcastically. "Just some thugs who tried to steal our luggage and a guide who was going to let them."

Bidai's eyes narrowed at the last remark.

"Oh, dear," Wilson said with obvious concern. "Were they successful?"

"No," Frank answered as he stepped into the small room. He had no interest in discussing the attack further. In front of him was a clear plastic tent completely enclosing a hospital bed. In the bed was Fenton Hardy, his eyes closed, sweat beaded on his forehead. A short, dark-haired woman was on the far side of the bed taking Fenton's pulse. She wore a white lab coat, a surgical mask, and Latex gloves. When she saw the boys, she backed out of the tent and pulled off the mask and gloves, tossing them in a basket.

"Dr. Tokunaga, Bidai has returned with Joe and Frank Hardy," Thomas said.

Dr. Tokunaga ignored them as she made notes on a clipboard. Inside the tent, Fenton was breathing rapidly. Even with the plastic curtains between them, Joe and Frank could hear his wheezing.

The guys stared as Fenton mumbled something

23

and tossed his head violently. Neither could make out their father's words.

"He's been mumbling incoherently for two days," Dr. Tokunaga said, finally speaking to them. "I'm afraid he's going downhill."

"Dad," Joe called, stepping close to the tent. "Dad, can you hear me? It's Joe."

Fenton continued to toss his head and mumble. Joe reached for the plastic and began pulling it away to get closer to his father. But Thomas grabbed his wrist and stopped him.

"He's in quarantine," Dr. Tokunaga said firmly. "He may be contagious. You must not open the tent."

Frank put his hand on Joe's shoulder to steady him, and the two watched their father helplessly.

Dr. Tokunaga searched their faces, her expression cold. The silence was broken by the creak of the door behind them. A small native woman, also dressed in white, fluttered a note into the room from the doorway. Realizing that she didn't want to enter the quarantined cubicle, Frank took the note.

"For Bidai," she said, and quickly closed the door again.

Frank looked at the note. He couldn't read it, of course, but did make out the number twelve and memorized the shape of the words. Then he passed the paper to Bidai, who read the note with a small smile slipping over his lips. He stuffed the note into his pocket and again focused on the weak Fenton Hardy.

"What do you mean he's going downhill?" Joe demanded, ignoring the interruption.

Dr. Tokunaga had folded her arms around the clipboard she held flat against her. "Both his heart and breathing rate have increased today," she said, without emotion. "He came here three days ago very ill but conscious. We thought he had picked up some fever in the jungle and that, with treatment, it would pass. But nothing we have tried has done any good."

"Don't you have any idea what's wrong with him?" Joe asked, desperation sounding in his voice.

"I told you we don't," she said with an authoritative air that indicated she didn't like being questioned.

"But what about the insect bite?" Thomas offered, speaking for the first time since they'd entered the room.

Dr. Tokunaga shot her assistant a vicious look, her eyes flashing. "I told you it's meaningless," she said. "There are no insects whose poison could cause the symptoms he has."

"What insect bite?" Joe asked, sensing that Dr. Tokunaga was protesting too much.

The doctor glared at Thomas before motioning toward Fenton's head. "There, on his neck."

When Joe and Frank stepped closer to the plastic tent, they could see a red circle with a dot like a puncture wound just below their father's ear.

Joe moved to the head of the bed. Frank started to step closer, as well, but stopped when he saw Bidai's eyes. They were open wide in a look that Frank interpreted as a combination of surprise and fear.

Bidai took a step backward, pressing himself against the wall of the room. "Excuse me," he whispered, then quickly slipped through the door.

Frank followed Bidai into the hall and grabbed him by the shoulder. "Is something wrong?" he asked, spinning Bidai around to face him.

"No, nothing," Bidai insisted, pulling away from Frank. "I just needed some air."

"You saw something in there that scared you," Frank continued. He pushed Bidai against the wall and braced himself for a showdown.

Bidai raised his chin defiantly, and for a moment Frank thought he would fight. Then the Iban's eyes softened and his body relaxed slightly.

"I will tell you," he said. "But you must keep it to yourself. I do not want my tribe blamed for your father's illness."

"Okay," Frank promised, stepping back a little to give Bidai some breathing room.

"The spot could be a bug bite," Bidai said. "But it is also like that made by a dart, and the placement, right below the ear, is exactly where a good marksman would aim."

Frank was confused, then remembered something Joe had said about the Borneo natives and how they hunted.

"You think my father was shot with a blowpipe?" he asked.

"Maybe," Bidai said, frowning.

"Then it could be a poison dart that made him sick," Frank said, watching Bidai's eyes. "But how serious could that be?"

"The early European explorers feared poison darts more than the bite of a king cobra," Bidai said. "Iban poison is always fatal."

Chapter

4

"If Dad's been poisoned, we have to tell the doctor," Joe said from behind Frank. He had walked up behind his brother in time to hear what Bidai had said.

"But your father would have been dead within minutes from Iban poison," Bidai said, shaking his head. "If it was a dart that hit Mr. Hardy, its tip was treated with something else."

"But what?" Frank asked.

Bidai shrugged, then looked down at his feet as the door to Fenton's room opened again and Dr. Tokunaga and Thomas stepped out.

Frank frowned. He had promised to keep Bidai's suspicions secret, but he had to help his father. He followed Dr. Tokunaga down the hall, with Joe beside him.

"Doctor," Frank said when they were away from Bidai. "Could it be a poison that's making Dad sick? Maybe from a plant?"

"Or dart," Joe added. He had made no promise to Bidai.

Dr. Tokunaga stopped and frowned deeply. "No local poisons would cause your father's symptoms," she said flatly, and continued down the hall.

"What now?" Joe asked no one in particular, and sighed.

"Let's find Dad's luggage," Frank suggested after a moment of thought. "Maybe he has some papers explaining the case he was on. But first I want to ask that nurse to translate the note she gave to Bidai."

Down the hall Joe watched Dr. Tokunaga give Thomas some instructions. Then she stepped inside her office and closed the door. Thomas walked back toward Joe, smiling apologetically.

"She's a regular Jack Frost, isn't she?" he said, shaking his head.

"But she is a good doctor, right?" Joe asked anxiously.

"Oh, yes. She's just not open to suggestions," Thomas said with a shrug, then touched Joe on the shoulder. "Anything I can do for you?"

"Tell us where our dad's belongings are," Joe said, pushing his hands in the pockets of his shorts.

"I don't know," Thomas replied. "He brought nothing with him."

"Maybe his luggage is still at his hotel," Bidai said. He and Frank had rejoined Joe and Thomas. "The White Hornbill, probably—most tourists stay there. I'll take you."

"Hornbill." Frank repeated the word under his breath. The nurse had translated into English—for a small fee—what he remembered had been on the note. It translated, "Hornbill, twelve midnight. We'll try again." Could Bidai's partners have guessed they would go to the hotel and planned another ambush?

Frank hated to get back in a car with Bidai and thought about pulling his brother aside to talk. But there was no place they could talk in private.

"You've done enough for us already," Frank finally said. "Maybe we can get a cab."

Thomas smiled patiently. "Bidai's car is a cab," he said. "He can help you check in. Someone will call you at the hotel if there's any change in your father."

"He's right," Joe told his brother. "We can't do anything here anyway."

Frank nodded, then followed his brother and Bidai out of the building.

"Bet there are things you'd rather be doing tonight, Bidai," Frank said lightly as they climbed into the car.

"Not till later," Bidai said with a smile. "I have big plans later—with a very special bird."

Frank returned his smile, wondering if the bird was a hornbill. The roar of the engine made it impossible for him to ask any more questions as the car sped down the bumpy street.

A few minutes later Bidai parked the car in front of one of the few modern-looking buildings on the edge of a business district that covered the equivalent of about two city blocks.

A sign said the building was the White Hornbill Hotel. It was two stories high and constructed of heavy mahogany timbers and red tiles. An open-air restaurant with a thatched roof was attached to the side of the hotel.

Bidai hopped out of the car and opened the door for the Hardys, then grabbed their bags and led the way to the entrance.

The heavy hardwood door swung open in front of them, and two smiling young men came out to take the bags. They had the same dark skin as Bidai, and Joe noticed that both made small bows to Bidai. Frank and Joe walked to the mahogany reception desk where a sign said English Spoken Here. An elderly man there also gave Bidai a respectful nod.

"Don't tell me, they're all Iban," Joe whispered to Bidai.

"Yes," Bidai said proudly. "They'll take good care of you."

"Am I mistaken, or are they all bowing to

you?" Frank asked, suddenly wondering if he could trust any of them.

Bidai laughed. "You are very observant, Frank Hardy. You should be a detective."

Before either Frank or Joe could comment, Bidai had headed back toward the door with the youngest of the bellhops.

"Room for two?" the smiling Iban clerk asked from behind the desk.

Frank and Joe turned to face him and saw that he was holding out a key to them.

"Yes," Frank said, taking it. "And I'd like to get my father's belongings. He stayed here a few days ago. His name is Fenton Hardy."

The clerk turned and talked quietly to one of the bellhops, who nodded and then shrugged.

"I remember Mr. Hardy," the clerk said, turning back to the boys. "His things are stored in a closet, but only the day maid has a key. You'll have to wait until tomorrow."

Joe didn't want to wait but had no choice. A bellhop grabbed their bags and led them up the heavy staircase and along a narrow hallway to a small corner room overlooking the street.

As soon as the bellhop was gone, Frank began searching the room.

"Is there something I don't know about?" Joe asked as he watched his brother peer under the bed.

"I think we might be in another ambush,"

32

Frank said, checking the one small closet. He told Joe about the note to Bidai.

"Hornbill, midnight," Joe repeated thought-fully. "Then the important plans that Bidai had for later tonight could be to come back here and rob us after we're asleep."

"That's the way I figure it," Frank said, check-ing under the second bed. "The 'very special bird' he mentioned could be the Hornbill Hotel. And we could be sitting ducks."

"No one knew we'd come here."

"Yeah, but remember Bidai suggested it," Frank said, feeling around the windowsill for electronic bugs. "The clerks could be in on it, too."

"Yeah," Joe said, joining Frank's search. He felt around the edges of the two nightstands and lifted up both lamps, examining the bottoms.

Frank checked the small table and chairs by the window, then sat on the bed nearest the door. He'd made a full circle of the room and found nothing.

"Any ideas what those guys might have been trying to steal from us?" Joe asked, slumping into a chair across from him.

"Just one," Frank said, touching the money belt around his waist. "The map."

"Which has to have something to do with Dad's case," Joe commented. "I wish we knew more about it. It must be something big."

"And dangerous," Frank added. He glanced at

his watch. It was 10:00 P.M. They had time for a late dinner before their midnight "appointment."

Joe called room service and asked what they had that was like burgers and fries. The guys settled on satay and nasi goreng. When the food arrived, it turned out to be beef shish kebabs with peanut sauce.

"At least they're feeding us well," Frank commented, finishing the meal.

"Yeah, let's just hope they're not fattening us up for the slaughter," Joe added, checking his watch.

At 11:30 Joe stationed himself beside the door to the room, and Frank sat on the edge of one of the two beds, keeping an eye on the front of the hotel.

Nothing happened.

"I'm starting to think the note didn't have anything to do with us," Frank said as his digital watch flicked to 12:30.

"Or maybe they stayed away because they knew we'd be ready," Joe suggested, cracking the door to take one final glance down the hall. "Your intercepting that note might have saved us a lot of trouble."

"Maybe," Frank agreed. He turned from the window and stretched out on the bed. "Let's get some rest. We'll do more digging tomorrow."

"Let's just hope we find something out," Joe murmured as he hit the lights. "We've traveled halfway around the world; Dad is dying; and our only clue is a map we don't understand."

As the guys knelt over Fenton Hardy's worn leather suitcases the next morning, they were quiet and somber. Joe had called the hospital as soon as he woke and learned that his father's condition was unchanged. Then he and Frank had retrieved their dad's luggage. The bags were their only hope for a clue.

Frank and Joe each opened a suitcase, hesitating for a fraction of a second before starting. Joe touched the brown shaving kit they had given Fenton one Christmas. Frank carefully removed a family picture Fenton always carried, then emptied his dad's hard-sided case. He felt along the inside edges, found the hidden button he knew was there, and pushed it. There was a muffled pop, and the bottom panel of the suitcase came up about an inch. Frank eased his fingers under the edge of it and lifted the thin piece of wood revealing a large secret compartment with two manila envelopes inside.

Joe knelt beside his brother. Each of them took an envelope, tore it open, and began to pore over the contents.

"According to this, Dad came to Borneo to find an old laboratory built by the Japanese during the Second World War," Frank said in awe. "The lab was hidden in the jungle someplace near the Rajang River. Phillips Pharmaceuticals got hold of recently declassified government documents saying the lab may have contained a biologically engineered strain of anthrax called anthrax-B."

"I've got a magazine article here that mentions it," Joe said, smoothing the yellowed papers on the bed. "But it doesn't explain why Phillips is interested in anthrax. Isn't that a disease cattle get?"

"Cattle, sheep, rabbits—according to this, most mammals, including humans, can catch it from one another or from bacteria in the air or soil. And it's very deadly," Frank explained after he'd read the article. "Apparently various anthrax bacteria were stored away by both sides in World War Two for use as biological weapons. And here's the kicker—the bacteria can survive for decades. Phillips seems to think that some anthrax-B might still be alive in the abandoned Japanese laboratory."

"But why would they want anthrax-B? I thought Phillips was into finding cures, not diseases," Joe said, sitting on the bed.

"They are." Frank put his papers down and stared at his brother thoughtfully. "But according to a memo they sent Dad, Phillips thinks the Japanese also developed a simple, fast cure for anthrax-B. That way the Japanese could use anthrax-B on their enemies and still protect their own people. Phillips hired Dad to find the cure because the company's research department thinks it might work on other strains of anthrax, too—meaning it would be worth millions."

"That explains why Dad also had this article," Joe said, pulling several pages clipped together out of the pile of documents on the bed. "It's an interview with an ex-marine named Jack Mulvaney, from a 1954 issue of *Wild Things* magazine. He talks about seeing a pair of clouded leopards here in Borneo when he was running from the Japanese during the war—after he and some other guys had found a hidden laboratory."

As Frank listened, Joe began to read part of the story recounted by Mulvaney.

" 'Dr. Joseph Whitefeather and I were doing reconnaissance when we stumbled onto a Japanese laboratory. It was pure luck that we found it since it was in a small cave and vines had been trained to grow over the front. It appeared deserted, but when we walked inside we found the place full of lab equipment and test tubes. Dr. Whitefeather could read Japanese and became very excited about one rack of glass vials. He tucked one inside his pack. I couldn't get him to leave, so I waited outside and yelled when I saw soldiers coming. We had to run for it. Whitefeather got out of the lab and headed south. I was headed north with Japanese soldiers on my tail when I practically tripped over a clouded leopard and her kitten. She was so mad, she attacked the next thing that ran by, which was one of the Japanese soldiers—probably saved my life.' "

Joe stopped reading and scanned the rest of the article. "It's all about the leopards after that. Nothing more about Whitefeather or the test tube."

Frank sighed. "Here's a report from Phillips about anthrax-B," he said, holding up a sheet of paper from near the bottom of his stack. "The disease causes high fever, rapid breathing, and an accelerated heart rate."

Frank stopped long enough to note the recognition in Joe's eyes.

"Those are the same symptoms Dad has," Joe said slowly. "Do you think he could have found the anthrax-B and gotten sick from it."

"Let's hope not," Frank said quietly. "Because according to this, those symptoms are always followed within seven days by convulsions and death."

Chapter

5

"SEVEN DAYS," Joe repeated. They'd had dead-lines before but never with stakes like this.

"Dad checked into the hospital four days ago," Frank reminded him.

Joe shook his head slowly. "Meaning we have three days to find the cure. I guess we'd better get started."

Frank had already pulled out his shirttail and was unzipping the money belt around his waist.

"I guess this is the best clue we've got so far," he said, lifting the yellowed map carefully out of the pocket.

"Do you suppose one of the x's is the location of the lab?" Joe asked, helping Frank smooth out the map on the bed nearest the door.

"Maybe," Frank said. "But if one x is the lab, which one? And what's the other x?"

"I don't know, but we're going to need a guide to check out both places," Joe replied.

"Yeah, but not Bidai," Frank said firmly. "I still don't trust him. He led us into an ambush last night, and he weasels out of questions—like why the clerks all bowed to him."

"Yeah, and what his plans were last night."

Just then there was a knock on the door. Frank quickly tucked the map back in his belt, pulling his shirt over it before Joe opened the door.

"Good morning," a smiling Bidai sang out. "Where would you like to go today?"

"In your dreams," Joe said, standing in the doorway to block Bidai's way. "We went with you yesterday and almost lost our luggage."

"But, Joe," Bidai pleaded, "compared to your safety, luggage isn't important."

"It is to us," Joe said.

Bidai's smile faded as Joe closed the door in his face.

"Way to tell him," Frank said. He was already stuffing Fenton's clothes back in the suitcase. Meanwhile, Joe returned the two manila envelopes to the secret compartment beneath the false bottom of the case. Then the boys put Fenton's luggage in the closet and headed down to the lobby.

"We need to hire a guide," Frank said, resting his right forearm on the reception desk.

The clerk looked confused. "Bidai was just here."

"We'd prefer someone else," Joe said, stepping up beside his brother.

The clerk widened his eyes, then shrugged. "Bidai is a great guide and warrior. If he cannot help you—there is no one."

Joe could see the man wasn't going to budge. "Then where can we rent a car? We ought to be able to find our way around by ourselves."

The clerk laughed sarcastically and said, "Kijang is a small city. There are no cars to rent. You may walk if you wish, but please do not enter the jungle alone. Ibans get tired of rescuing tourists who get lost in the jungle."

Joe started to protest, but Frank touched his arm and motioned him away from the desk to a quiet corner of the lobby.

"We should have known these Ibans wouldn't help us," Joe grumbled. "I'll bet they were all in on Bidai's plans to steal our things. They probably even shot Dad with a dart."

"Maybe," Frank said, frowning. "But one thing's for sure—we don't have time to walk every place we have to go. Dad's life is at stake."

"Yeah, but you're not suggesting we get back in the car with that maniac driver, are you?" Joe said. Then lowering his voice further, he growled, "Great warrior—who does that clerk think he's kidding?"

"Look, we don't know that Bidai's done anything wrong," Frank reasoned. "And even if he was in on the ambush, it would be better to have him with us instead of sneaking around behind us."

Joe rolled his eyes and let out a slow sigh. "I guess. But I still don't like it."

Frank slapped his brother on the back and walked back to the desk. "You talked us into it," he said to the clerk. "We'll hire Bidai."

With a look of satisfaction, the clerk nodded, and the bellhop nearest the front door stepped outside. A minute later Bidai walked into the lobby, all smiles.

The idea that Bidai had been waiting outside only increased Joe's fears about him.

"I charge forty dollars a day," Bidai said boldly, holding out his hand.

"Forty dollars!" Joe said, raising his eyebrows. "Isn't that about a month's wages in Kijang?"

"Agreed," Frank said quickly, shaking Bidai's hand.

"In advance," Bidai added, still smiling.

Joe groaned as Frank dug out his wallet and handed Bidai two twenties.

"Where to?" Bidai asked brightly as he stuffed the bills into his pocket.

"The hospital," Frank answered, walking to the car.

The streets were crowded with morning shoppers, and Bidai had to drive slowly. In daylight Kijang was a lively place. The streets were lined with small shops, their doors open and owners beckoning customers inside.

Sweat was again rolling off Frank and Joe as Bidai's open-air car bounced along. Once they were out of the business district, Bidai covered the last few blocks to the hospital with a short burst of speed.

"I will be back in an hour to get you," Bidai said as the guys vaulted out of the car.

"Hey, we paid for the whole day," Joe protested, but Frank grabbed his brother's arm and nodded to Bidai. He couldn't blame their guide for wanting to avoid a second visit to a man with a deadly—and possibly contagious—disease.

Fenton was still unconscious, resting quietly inside the tent.

"He looks almost normal," Frank said sadly.

"Yeah, like he should just wake up and walk out of here," Joe murmured. "I've never felt so helpless." Frustrated, he hit the wall with a palm.

Frank gently touched his brother on the shoulder and turned him toward the door.

In the hallway they spotted Dr. Tokunaga going into a room and followed her.

"We want you to test Dad for anthrax-B," Frank said when they were inside the shelf-lined room that was obviously a lab. They were standing at the end of a counter, Dr. Tokunaga across from Thomas.

Frank thought he saw Dr. Tokunaga tense

when she heard the word *anthrax,* but she quickly regained her composure.

"Anthrax-B? What is that?" Thomas asked.

Dr. Tokunaga folded her arms. She looked totally calm, except for the fire building in her eyes.

"A biological weapon developed in World War Two," Joe said. "We think our dad may have been exposed to it."

"Nonsense," Dr. Tokunaga said, her voice perfectly steady. "There is no anthrax in Borneo. And I will not have you talking about it."

"We want the test done," Frank demanded again, leaning against the counter.

"It's a waste of time, and besides, it would take days to prepare a culture," Dr. Tokunaga said, still glaring.

"No, it won't," Thomas said quietly. "I can do it right now." He pretended to keep working on some slides, but he was watching the doctor out of the corner of his eye.

Dr. Tokunaga's back stiffened, and for a moment Frank thought she was going to lose her cool. Instead she took a deep breath and turned slowly to stare straight at Thomas. "That's twice you've contradicted me," she said, her voice an angry hiss. Then she turned and strode from the room.

"I suggested anthrax two days ago," Thomas said with a shrug. "Based strictly on the symptoms, of course. But Dr. Tokunaga got angry at my suggestion—even left the hospital for a couple of hours. She forbade me to do the tests. I did, however, prepare the cultures from some of the patient's blood. It will take only a few minutes to make the slides."

Joe and Frank watched anxiously as Thomas took a round glass petri dish from a small refrigerator. He put some of its clear contents on a microscope slide and then added a special colored solution. Then he slipped the slide into his microscope and, after several moments of careful scrutiny, raised his eyes.

"It's anthrax all right," he announced with a frown. "But different from any I've ever seen."

"Anthrax-B," Joe murmured. "But how did he get it?"

"Hard to say," Thomas said, shaking his head. "Anthrax is mostly contracted by breathing in the bacteria or through cuts in the skin."

Frank wondered immediately if Fenton had been infected by a poison dart.

"Do you often make your boss mad?" Joe asked Thomas as he labeled the slide.

"Oh, she's always mad about something," Thomas said with a grin. "But she does seem different on this case, almost like she doesn't want to find the cause of your father's illness."

"I think we'd better talk to her," Frank said, looking at Thomas. "Are you up to it?"

Thomas nodded and led the Hardys down the hall to a small office where Dr. Tokunaga sat at a polished mahogany desk. Everything in the room was clean and orderly. A bookcase on one wall held rows of medical references. The desk was clear except for some papers and two small coins.

Joe recognized them immediately. Marsha Bailey had brought some just like them to his social studies class. They were Pakistani rupees.

"It's anthrax-B," Frank announced firmly. "There must be some antibiotic you can try."

Dr. Tokunaga rubbed her temples in slow circles and then laced her fingers together underneath her chin.

"I have already tried antibiotics," she said quietly. "In fact, I have tried every one recommended for treating anthrax. Nothing works."

"Then you suspected anthrax all along?" Frank asked, his voice hard.

"Yes," Dr. Tokunaga said, focusing down on her desk. "But I think it was a mistake to confirm it. If the story gets out, it could be disastrous."

Frank and Joe both had puzzled expressions.

"The Ibans here are deathly afraid of anthrax," Dr. Tokunaga explained. "During the war, the Japanese used it to kill three-fourths of the tribe. Then they gave the Ibans a cure in exchange for a promise to stop killing Japanese soldiers with their blowpipes. If the Ibans hear that anthrax-B has reappeared, we could be flooded with people certain they have the disease. Our small facility couldn't handle that, and people who really are sick wouldn't be able to get help. Besides that,"

Dr. Tokunaga said, pushing her chin out a little and staring straight at the guys, "they might blame me."

It took Joe and Frank a minute to understand that Dr. Tokunaga feared she'd become a scapegoat, since she herself was Japanese.

"But what about the cure?" Frank demanded. "You said the soldiers had a cure."

"They gave the Ibans a greenish liquid to drink. It made them well, but no one knows what was in it. It's one of Borneo's mysteries."

For a tense moment Frank and Joe were speechless.

"There is one person who might know something," Thomas offered. He was standing, leaning against the wall of the office and listening quietly. As he spoke, he stepped forward, only to be stopped by Dr. Tokunaga's angry eyes once again.

"You will not speak of this anymore," she ordered stonily. "Now, get out of my office—all of you."

"Just a minute," Frank cut in. "You can't just shove this under the rug. Not when my father's life is a stake."

"What do you want me to do?" Dr. Tokunaga snapped.

"Try to find the cure," Joe blurted, raising his hands in frustration.

"There is no cure," Dr. Tokunaga said, rising to her feet. "Now, if you'll excuse me, I've had enough of this nonsense." She stepped past them all and walked out.

No one in the office moved for several seconds.

"His name's Jungle Mulvaney," Thomas said at last, answering Frank and Joe's question before they had time to ask. "Or at least that's what the people call him. He stayed here after the war. Apparently he's into orchids—they grow well here. He's an odd bird, kind of a hermit who lives in the jungle north of here, but he doesn't mind people as long as they don't bother his flowers. I've heard he has some strange stories to tell about the war."

Frank recognized the name Mulvaney and wondered if it was the same man interviewed for *Wild Things* magazine so many years ago.

"Why didn't Dr. Tokunaga want you to tell us about him?" Frank asked, sinking into a chair.

"Beats me," Thomas said with a shrug. "She's strangely touchy about this whole thing. You're lucky to have me around to be sure your father gets proper care. Personally, I don't trust—"

His words were interrupted by a loud crash and the sound of shattering glass.

Frank and Joe jumped toward the office door. As Joe pulled it open, they heard Dr. Tokunaga yell, "Thief, thief!"

They stepped into the hall and saw her running toward them from the hospital lab, blood splattered on her white coat.

Chapter
6

"IN THE LAB!" Dr. Tokunaga shouted when she saw the Hardys. "There's a burglar!"

The guys rushed past her with Joe in the lead. They barreled through the doorway to find the lab deserted but a mess. The counter where Thomas and Dr. Tokunaga worked had been overturned. The microscope lay on the floor, bent and broken. Test tubes and slides had shattered, splattering blood samples across the polished hardwood. And in the rear, an open window let in the steamy jungle air.

"There was a man looking through the samples," Dr. Tokunaga cried as she caught up with the Hardys. "The thief was there, next to the refrigerator."

"What did he look like?" Frank asked, scanning the ransacked office.

"I didn't get a good look," Dr. Tokunaga said. "As soon as I came in, he pulled a shield in front of his face—an Iban shield, the kind they used to take into battle. I don't even recall what he was wearing—a light blue shirt, maybe. There was just a flash of color before he pulled up the shield. Then he pushed the counter over and ran to the window."

"Was he Iban?" Joe asked coolly.

"I suppose," Dr. Tokunaga said, a hint of despair in her voice. "Anyway, the shield was."

"But what would an Iban want to steal from your lab?" Frank asked skeptically.

"Maybe the test results on your father," Dr. Tokunaga said. "Maybe someone's out to discredit me."

The Hardys exchanged questioning glances. Dr. Tokunaga's eyes narrowed as she sensed their distrust. "Isn't it obvious someone was here?" she spat out. "Now, excuse me. I've got to change clothes."

"Let's have a look around," Frank said as Dr. Tokunaga hurried away.

The guys stepped carefully into the room, trying to avoid the glass and blood. The intruder had left no clues behind. As Frank leaned out the open window, Joe whispered in his ear, "Maybe the doctor staged this to destroy the evidence of anthrax."

"Could be," Frank agreed. "But if that's the

case, she did a good job. She even put tracks outside the window."

Frank stepped back to let Joe look. The tracks were barely visible in the dry dirt but definitely led from the window to the jungle just beyond.

"Do you think Dr. Tokunaga is right, that someone was here trying to steal the test results?" Frank asked, scanning the windowsill for evidence.

"I don't know," Joe said, heading for the door. "Maybe this Jungle Mulvaney guy will have some answers."

As Joe pushed open the hospital door, he nearly crashed into Bidai. The startled guide lost his smile for an instant, but then greeted the Hardys in his usual cheerful manner.

"I guess I got back just in time," Bidai said.

"So, where were you?" Frank asked.

Bidai's smile only broadened. "Making very important preparations for a party," he said. "But now I'll take you anywhere you wish." He raised his hands skyward in a gesture that offered the guys the universe.

Frank frowned, then said, "We want to visit Jungle Mulvaney. Do you know him?"

"Ooooh, yes," Bidai said, raising his eyebrows. "The crazy American who lives in the trees. Does he know something about your father's sickness?"

"Maybe," Joe answered, and started quickly

toward the open-topped car. He didn't want to tell Bidai anymore.

"How about some lunch?" Bidai asked brightly as he started the engine. "The market is on the way."

"Okay," Frank said, swinging into the front seat beside Bidai. "But let's make it quick."

Fortunately, the market was only a few minutes away. Bidai pulled the car onto the dirt shoulder of the street in front of a row of food booths. He suggested one that served a dish of fried noodles and pork called roast babi. It was served on thin paper plates, and they took theirs with them to eat in the car.

Bidai's driving was even more reckless when he had food in one hand. The car careened along a rutted, dusty road that wound through the jungle. Ancient trees towered above them with huge trunks and branches that intertwined above the road, forming a canopy that blocked out the sun.

One big bump nearly sent Frank's plate flying off his lap. At the same time, he felt something brush against his foot. He glanced down and saw a shield that had bounced out from under the seat.

Frank felt his heart skip a beat. He wondered if it was the same shield Dr. Tokunaga had seen in the lab, and if Bidai had been the person behind it. If so, they could be heading into another ambush.

Frank peeked at Bidai to see if he had noticed,

but the driver's eyes were focused on the road. After silently pointing the shield out to Joe, Frank slid it back under the seat with his foot.

After twenty minutes Bidai veered off the road, heading across a small clearing at breakneck speed. Just as the car was about to slam into a huge tree, Bidai slammed on the brakes.

"We walk from here," he announced.

Frank glanced at Joe. If Bidai wanted to set up another ambush, this would be a perfect spot.

"Are you sure this is the way to Mulvaney's?" Joe asked, eyeing the thick jungle cautiously.

"I am sure," Bidai said with a grin. "When I was a boy, my friends and I used to hide outside his tree house and watch him talk to flowers."

"Stay alert," Frank whispered to Joe.

Joe frowned. The jungle was dark and threatening even at midday. The chatter of gibbons punctuated the skittering sounds of creatures scurrying up and down tree trunks.

Bidai led them along a narrow path that was cut tunnel-like through the jungle. From the towering hardwood trees and vines above, exotic flowers dangled in their faces. Hundreds of different kinds of birds sang from hiding places in the dense greenery.

After several minutes Bidai stopped.

"Here we are," he said, "at the sandalwood tree."

Frank and Joe gazed in the direction of his outstretched hand, their eyes traveling up the trunk of the broad tree, its branches reaching out in every direction above them.

"A tree house," Frank cried in amazement. The tree was dotted with a series of small bamboo huts, like a Christmas tree full of ornaments. The large branches served as walkways between them. Each hut had a window opening and a roof thatched with huge leaves from the tree, making it hard to pick out the structures from the foliage.

Frank sized up the unusual jungle house. There were no steps or ladders, and the nearest structure was a small platform ten feet above their heads.

"Hello," Frank yelled, cupping his hands around his mouth. "Anybody home?"

A moment later a fair-skinned man with a red beard stepped onto a narrow walkway outside one of the highest huts. He peered at them for a moment and then started down the tree, moving so smoothly along the thick tree limbs that he reminded Frank and Joe of a monkey. Several times he completely disappeared behind clumps of leaves, but in less than a minute, he was standing on the small platform above them.

Frank introduced himself, Joe, and Bidai. "We'd like to talk to you," he yelled into the tree.

"What about?" Mulvaney asked. His bushy red mustache twitched.

Frank explained who they were and asked if Mulvaney knew their father. "Can we come up?"

Mulvaney rubbed his beard thoughtfully.

"Yeah, I suppose," he said at last. "But be careful of the orchids. They're fragile."

He lowered a bamboo and vine ladder, and the Hardys followed Bidai up the ladder and then continued to climb as Mulvaney led the way to one of the huts near the top of the tree. They were careful not to crush the brilliant lavender orchids that vined around the trunk. Joe did pause to sniff one and found that it smelled like vanilla.

"This is my workshop," Mulvaney said as he led them into the hut where they had first seen him. "Watch out, though," he warned, pointing to Joe's hand.

Joe pulled his hand back just before it brushed a delicate orchid growing in a woven basket hung beside the doorway. Inside, Joe and Frank huddled close to the small window. From there they could see the jungle's canopy stretching out like monkey bars, but this jungle gym was made of twisting, living plants.

Frank jumped as a bright red parrot flew up just a few feet from the window, then disappeared into the foliage.

"What exactly can I do for you?" Mulvaney asked, seating himself on a wooden stool. A small shelf beside him was filled with carved figurines of all sorts of animals. At the opposite end of the hut was a pile of wood. Mulvaney grabbed a piece and began carving it with a pocketknife while Frank explained about Fenton's illness, the article, and their need to find a cure for anthrax-B.

"Are you the Jack Mulvaney who found the Japanese lab during the war?" Joe asked, finally stepping back from the window.

He watched as Mulvaney cleaned under a fingernail with the knife. Joe guessed he had to be at least seventy-five years old. His skin was wrinkled and leathery, but he appeared healthy and fit.

"Yeah, we found the lab while doing recon and making maps of the Rajang River area, but I don't know much about anthrax-B, except that Dr. Whitefeather seemed to be all excited about having a cure. Of course, he died for his trouble."

Bidai squatted patiently in a corner of the hut, perfectly balanced with no apparent need to stretch or move.

Mulvaney kept talking and carving until his piece of wood took the shape of a monkey. The tale he told was basically the same one the magazine article had reported, but Mulvaney told it with the broad hand gestures and exaggerated expressions of an expert storyteller.

"So Whitefeather had the cure when he left the lab?" Joe asked when Mulvaney paused.

"He said he did," Mulvaney answered, squinting as though he were giving a great deal of thought to the question. "I had trouble getting him to leave the lab. He got real excited about a set of glass vials in a tray labeled in Japanese. That's when he said he had a cure for anthrax and put one of the vials in his pack. Then we heard someone coming and took off running. Whitefeather ran the other way."

"And Whitefeather didn't make it out?" Frank asked, folding his arms.

Mulvaney shook his head, then made a motion toward the ceiling with his knife. "He put up a signal flare that night, and I marked his location on a map, but it took me two days to get back to our unit. The rescue team that was sent out never found him. Never located the lab again, either." He smiled. "Things tend to disappear in the jungle."

"What happened to the map?" Joe asked.

Mulvaney rocked back on his stool and took a few more swipes at the wood with his knife.

"I copied it when I got back and turned it over to my commander. Kept the rough copy myself until last week, when I ran into your dad and gave him my copy."

For a moment neither Joe nor Frank moved. Then Frank slowly got to his feet and pulled out the map.

"Is this it?" he asked.

"It sure is," Mulvaney said, taking the yellow paper.

He pointed to the x closest to the Rajang River. "This is the location of the secret lab. The other x is where I saw Whitefeather's flare."

Mulvaney handed the map back to Frank.

"Of course, you'll never find anything at either spot now. The critters carry off anything that's edible, and the vines and ferns cover everything else," Mulvaney said matter-of-factly. "I told your dad that, but he wanted to look anyway. I suppose you will, too."

"Maybe," Joe said, not wanting to say anything in front of Bidai.

The Hardys thanked Mulvaney and got up to leave.

"Tell me," Mulvaney said, putting his carving on the shelf and following them outside the hut. "Why all the interest in anthrax all of a sudden? This is the third time I've been asked about it."

Frank and Joe exchanged glances.

"There was someone here besides our dad and us?" Joe asked, surprised.

"Yeah, some doctor was here last Saturday afternoon," he said. "She asked the same questions as you."

Frank and Joe tried not to show their dismay. Apparently, Dr. Tokunaga was one step ahead of them.

Jungle Mulvaney seemed mildly disappointed when they said they were ready to leave. He led them down the tree, having to wait occasionally while they caught up.

Once on the ground, Bidai walked confidently into the jungle with Joe and Frank behind him. They were quiet as they moved through the tunnel-like pathway, again alert to the potential for ambush.

Ahead of them, Bidai slipped easily through the passage, without even rustling the leaves. Joe had just ducked under a low branch and was hurrying to keep Bidai in sight when he heard a muffled shout.

He turned and saw the branch he had just ducked under shaking violently. A huge python hung from the limb, its brown and black spots undulating like trembling leaves. It was coiled around something, its body still moving into position to crush its prey. As the coils parted for a moment, Joe could make out Frank's face, twisted in agony. Frank would be crushed in a matter of seconds.

Chapter

7

THE SNAKE'S TAIL was still wrapped tightly around the branch, but the rest of its body was coiled around Frank. It had to be at least twenty feet long. Joe knew pythons were deadly, even though they weren't poisonous—they killed by suffocating their victims and eating them whole.

Joe checked the ground for something to use as a weapon. He grabbed a wedge-shaped rock. As he approached the snake, he searched for the creature's head, finally spotting it near Frank's knees, its short teeth clamped onto Frank's leg.

Joe banged the rock down hard on the snake's angular head, and the python immediately removed its teeth from Frank. Its bright eyes refocused on Joe, who swung the rock again. This time the python dodged, and Joe's arm swept harmlessly through the air. The python struck back, grabbing Joe's wrist. As its teeth sank into his flesh, Joe yelled and dropped the rock.

Joe threw himself backward with all his might, wrenching free from the snake. The python was still coiled tightly around his brother, and Joe could tell that Frank was running out of time. Then, as Joe tumbled into the bushes, blood trickling from the shallow gashes in his arm, he saw Bidai reappear along the narrow path with a large hunting knife in his hand.

Bidai leaped toward the snake, slashing at it with his knife. With two quick strokes, he severed the head, and the python went limp, releasing its hold on the branch above and tumbling to the ground with Frank still inside its coiled body.

Joe was on his feet in an instant, helping Bidai untwist the heavy snake, then grabbing Frank's shoulders and pulling him free.

Frank took a huge, gasping breath, and Joe sank to the ground beside him. "I thought you were a goner," he said, his hand on Frank's shoulder.

Frank nodded in agreement and sucked in more air. Joe knew it would be several moments before he could speak. For now, it was enough to see him breathing.

Joe turned to Bidai, who was crouched in the narrow pathway, watching the two of them. His smile was gone, and Joe thought that for the first time, Bidai seemed concerned.

"Why didn't you call me?" Bidai asked, more hurt than angry. "You should have called as soon as you saw the snake."

Joe hesitated. He hadn't thought of yelling for Bidai, and he didn't want to tell the guide why. He did realize that Bidai had saved both of their lives, though. "I guess you're right" was all Joe could say.

Frank was breathing easier now. He sat with his arms around his knees, watching his brother.

"It's okay," Bidai said with a shrug.

"Anyway, thanks," Joe said. Staring at the ground, he added, "Maybe I've misjudged you."

Bidai looked hurt, but not surprised. "You were just upset because I didn't fight for your luggage," the young Iban said, smiling a little. "I understand, but it doesn't make much sense to me. You Americans care too much about things that don't matter. Here in Borneo we get by with very little."

"But you still like money," Joe said with a laugh, remembering Bidai's forty-dollar guide fee.

Bidai's smile widened. He shook his finger at Joe. "That's for the party," he said.

"What party?" Frank asked, finally joining the conversation.

"My eighteenth birthday," Bidai answered, his chest swelling with pride. "In just two weeks. The whole tribe will celebrate."

Frank wondered if the birthday party could explain some of Bidai's actions over the past two days. "What was your midnight rendezvous at the White Hornbill?" he asked.

Bidai's smile faded. "You read my note," he said. "It wasn't the White Hornbill, it just said Hornbill—the bird. They have big bills like those of a toucan and have always been very important to my tribe. I found a hornbill's roost, and my friend Siba promised to help me steal feathers in the night."

"But why?" Joe asked, confused.

"I need them for my shield—to show I'm ready to be a man," Bidai said. "My tribe used to decorate shields with hair from the heads of enemies killed in battle. But when the missionaries came, we stopped head-hunting and started using hornbill feathers instead."

Suddenly Frank laughed. "Then the shield under the seat in your car is for the party, too?" he asked.

"Yes," Bidai replied, acting surprised.

"And you really weren't the burglar in the lab this morning?" Frank pressed.

"Of course not," Bidai replied, very much insulted.

Frank was silent for a moment, thinking that Bidai either was an incredible liar or was innocent of all the things they'd suspected him of doing. Frank guessed it was the latter. He looked at Joe, who winked.

"Bidai," Frank said thoughtfully. "We're going to need a guide to take us into the jungle, and the clerk at the White Hornbill said you're the best. Would you lead us?" Frank produced the map, giving Bidai a good look at it for the first time.

"We need to check out these two *x*'s," he went on, spreading the map on the ground.

Bidai leaned over and studied it for a moment. "That will be a hard trip," the guide said, frowning. "We'd have to take a boat upriver, then walk to these places. We will be gone three, maybe four days."

"But we don't have that long," Joe said, throwing up his hands. "Dad's not expected to live past Wednesday."

"That's the day after tomorrow," Bidai gasped. "We might be able to visit one spot by then, but not both."

"Then we'll visit the lab," Frank said, pointing to the *x* nearest the river. "It's our best hope."

"I'll take you there tomorrow," Bidai said, jumping to his feet. "Now help me with the snake." Then, seeing the questioning looks on their faces, he explained. "It is dinner for my whole tribe. You can come eat with us tonight. We'll celebrate tomorrow's trip."

Joe rolled his eyes as he and Frank got to their feet and each grabbed a section of the python. It took all three of them to carry the huge reptile on their shoulders. With Bidai in the lead, they headed through the jungle, the snake draped over them like a thick firehose.

*　　*　　*

It was late afternoon when Bidai dropped Joe and Frank off at the White Hornbill Hotel after taking them to check in at the hospital. Thomas was leaving Fenton's room when they arrived and told the Hardys their father's condition was unchanged. Frank thought his dad looked even paler than he had the last time they visited.

"I'll see you for dinner in an hour," Bidai said as the boys got out of the car. "You understand the way?"

"Yes," Frank told him. Bidai had instructed them carefully on the best way to walk to the longhouse, which was less than a mile from town.

Bidai waved as he drove off to deliver his python to the Iban cook.

The front door of the hotel swung open as Joe and Frank strode toward it. Inside, a young bellhop held the door, and a clerk with a name tag that said Inghai waved them in.

"A message for Mr. Hardy," he said, extending a small plain envelope.

Joe took it, thinking it must be a message from his mom. He ripped open the flap to find, instead, a note on white paper, scribbled in an unfamiliar hand.

"Leave the map at the desk or your father dies," it said.

"Who left this?" Joe demanded of the clerk, handing the note to Frank.

"I didn't get his name," the clerk said, concerned. "I've never seen him before. He came in and left the envelope and said there'd be a twenty-dollar tip when he got your reply."

"And when will he be back?" Frank asked, folding the note as he spoke.

"Around midnight," the clerk said, his eyes darting nervously between Frank and Joe.

"What did he look like?" Joe demanded. His knuckles were white from clenching the edge of the counter. He wanted to grab the clerk by the collar but reminded himself that the clerk was not his enemy. It was the man who delivered the note Joe needed to get his hands on.

"He wasn't Iban," the clerk said, sounding eager to be helpful. "And he wore a big hat pulled way down over his eyes."

"Are you going to be here at midnight?" Frank asked tensely.

"Yes," the clerk replied. "My shift ends at seven, but I planned to stay—to get the tip."

Frank sucked in a deep breath as he came up with a plan. "We'll give you twenty dollars more if you'll signal us when he comes in."

"What kind of signal?" the clerk asked, his gaze shifting from Frank to Joe.

Frank scanned the reception desk. His eyes stopped at the registration book. Next to it was a fancy pen in a holder.

"When you see him, move the pen set to the other side of the book," he said, demonstrating as he spoke. "I'll be watching."

The clerk nodded.

Frank peered deeply into the clerk's eyes, hoping he could trust him. After a moment he and Joe turned away and walked up the stairs to their room.

"At least we know one thing now," Joe said as he turned the key in the door of their room.

"What's that?" Frank asked as the door swung open.

"Someone wants that map—bad," Joe said, crossing the threshold. Frank followed him into the room and closed the door behind them. The shade was pulled, and the room was almost dark. As Joe reached for the light switch he heard a slight creak in the floorboards behind him.

"Frank, look ou—"

Joe's words were cut off as a strong hand clamped over his mouth and an arm closed around his throat.

Chapter

8

FRANK PEERED into the shadows, searching for the stranger behind his brother. The man was slightly shorter than Joe, with muscular arms. As he leaned out from behind Joe, Frank saw his face and balding head. It was the Gray Man, one of the top officials for the U.S. government spy agency called the Network.

"What are you doing here?" Frank gasped.

"The same thing you are," the Gray Man said, releasing Joe as he spoke. "Trying to save your father."

Joe flipped on the light switch and stood facing the secret agent.

"What do you know about Dad?" he asked, watching the Gray Man's eyes.

"I know he's in the hospital with a mysterious

disease," the Gray Man said calmly. "And that he's going to die unless you find a cure."

Frank knew the Gray Man wouldn't have come just to help them out. "What's your interest in this?" he asked suspiciously.

"I'm afraid you're not the only ones looking for the cure," the Gray Man said with a frown. "The Assassins are after it, too. If they find it first, your father will only be the first to die."

Joe stared at the floor. Knowing the Assassins, a group of fanatical terrorists working only for their own personal power, were involved made their dad's situation even more serious—and possibly hopeless.

"So it's the Assassins who've been hounding us," Frank said, a hint of despair in his voice. "But why are they interested in anthrax-B?"

The Gray Man raised his eyebrows. "Who told you it was anthrax-B?" he asked.

"We figured it out from Dad's papers," Joe said coolly. "And the lab assistant at the hospital confirmed it—or at least confirmed that it was a form of anthrax he had never seen before."

"Do you know where it came from?" the Gray Man asked, acting as if he hoped they didn't.

"A secret Japanese laboratory during World War Two," Joe said, matching the Gray Man's steely gaze. "It was developed as a biological weapon."

"But never used," the Gray Man said, his eyes narrowing.

"Except against the Iban natives," Frank said, folding his arms across his chest and feeling a little smug. He could see that the Gray Man hadn't expected them to know so much about the case. "And there was a cure—a greenish liquid that the Japanese gave the Ibans to drink."

The Gray Man stood and started slowly pacing away from the boys. Finally he spoke.

"Do you have a map?" he asked. Turning back toward them, he watched their faces carefully.

"First, tell us what the Assassins have to do with this," Joe said, sitting on the bed.

The Gray Man remained silent for a long moment. Frank guessed he was trying to decide how much to tell them.

"The Assassins have the anthrax-B bacteria," he said gravely. "They have a lab set up in the mountains of Pakistan where they're stockpiling the bacteria. But they want the cure."

Now that he had decided to level with them, his story came out easily.

"The Assassins aren't interested in just killing people with the bacteria," he said, shoving his hands into his pockets. "They see it as a business opportunity—a way to make money."

"Blackmail," Frank said, horrified. "If the Assassins have the cure, they can make people sick and then charge for the cure."

"That's right," the Gray Man said, folding his arms. "Anthrax is easy to spread. An airplane could dump it over a city. Our intelligence says that's exactly what the Assassins are planning to do. Anyone who breathes the air will get sick. Then the Assassins can charge millions of dollars for the cure."

Joe put his head in his hands and sighed. There was a sinking feeling in his stomach. "Then they're searching for the lab, too," he said. "Isn't that a long shot?"

The Gray Man nodded. "But the rewards are so high that they're willing to play the odds. Especially if they can get their hands on a map showing the location of the lab." He watched the boys' eyes. "I've heard that one was made—and I think you have it. I don't know why else the Assassins would be bothering you."

"What if we do?" Joe said defensively. "I hope you're not going to ask us to give it to you."

"Your father's life is at stake," the Gray Man said, sounding angry. "You can't expect to find the lab yourself. I can have a whole team on it within an hour after you give me the map. If there is a cure, I can get it to your father. Can you do that?"

"Maybe not," Frank said slowly. "But Dad needs more than the cure now. We just got a note saying that unless we turn the map over to some unknown person, he'll be murdered. We think the doctor may be one of the Assassins. She ordered her assistant not to test for anthrax, even when she recognized the symptoms. It's almost as if she wants Dad to die. If we give the map to you, will you protect our father?"

Joe glared at Frank. He had no intention of letting his brother turn over the map.

The Gray Man rubbed his chin thoughtfully.

"I'm not convinced the doctor is involved," he said. "As I understand it, she's been here for years, and unless she was recruited recently, we'd have her in our computer as an Assassin agent. But, yes, I do have a man who can protect your father."

Frank let out a sigh and began to pull his shirt-tail out, uncovering the money belt.

"Frank, no," Joe protested, pulling at his brother's arm.

"The Gray Man's right," Frank said. "The Network has a better chance of saving Dad than we do."

He unzipped the money belt and carefully withdrew the yellowed paper. "This is the map Jungle Mulvaney drew," he said, handing it to the Gray Man before Joe could stop him. "Now, how will we know this bodyguard, and when will he be at the hospital?"

As the Gray Man examined the map, the corner of his mouth turned up slightly.

"His name's Albert Garribay," the Gray Man said, tucking the map into his shirt. "He's big and blond, and he'll recognize you. Be in the lobby in ten minutes. By the way, you made the right decision."

The Gray Man turned and let himself out of the room.

"How could you give the map away?" Joe demanded when the door had closed behind Gray Man. "It was the only lead we had."

Frank smiled slyly and locked the door. Then, turning to Joe, he motioned with his finger for silence and unzipped the money belt a second time.

As Joe watched, Frank withdrew a second piece of paper, this one new and white. Joe saw that it was a copy of the map.

"I had this made at the airport when we were waiting for our plane," he said with satisfaction. "I thought it might come in handy. Now we have a map and a bodyguard for Dad. Plus, the Network is looking for the lab, too. I think things are definitely looking up."

Joe sprawled on the bed with the map in his hands.

"I've got an idea," he said, his fingers tracing the small x's on the map. "If the Network is going to look for the lab, why don't we concentrate on this other spot—Dr. Whitefeather's last known location. If he was well enough to send a signal, maybe he made a shelter or something. Maybe we can find the cure stashed there. We know he had it with him when he left the lab."

Frank frowned for a moment. According to Jungle Mulvaney, a search party had looked for Whitefeather fifty years ago and found nothing. Finding a vial in the jungle now had to be the king of long shots. Still, his brother was right—there was no point playing cleanup behind the Network.

"What about the midnight meeting?" Frank asked. "I think we should still try to catch this blackmailer, even if Dad has a bodyguard."

"Right," Joe agreed. "Maybe this guy will put the finger on Dr. Tokunaga."

"If I stand at the head of the staircase, I can see the desk clerk's signal," Frank said. "You wait in the alley across the street from the hotel. When the clerk moves the desk set, I'll run back to the room and blink my penlight in the window. That way, you'll know to follow the next person who walks out of the White Hornbill. I'll try to follow, too."

"We can leave an envelope with the clerk with a piece of paper in it," Joe said, studying the alley across the street. "He won't know when he leaves that we've double-crossed him."

Frank checked his watch. It was six o'clock. They had just half an hour to get to Bidai's longhouse. "Let's get that bodyguard up to Dad's room," he said.

There was only one man in the lobby who wasn't wearing a hotel uniform when Joe and Frank walked down the stairs. He was sitting in one of the big wicker chairs that lined the mahogany-paneled wall across from the desk. The man was blond, as the Gray Man had promised, and when the Hardys approached, he folded the newspaper, he'd been reading and stood up. He was at least six feet four with muscles swelling under his shirt sleeves.

"Al Garribay," the man said quietly, giving each of them a confident handshake. "I've got a vehicle outside. Shall we go?"

Joe raised his eyebrows in a signal of appreciation as Al turned to lead them toward the door. Frank smiled back. This man definitely was qualified to protect their father.

Network agents were always well briefed on their assignments, so the Hardys weren't surprised that Garribay knew the way to the Kijang hospital without directions.

"The Gray Man says I should pose as your cousin," Al said over his shoulder as he parked in the dirt lot. "If the Assassins have infiltrated the hospital, there's no sense letting them know the Network is here."

Al opened the hospital door and let Joe and Frank go in first. The hallway was empty.

Thomas was leaning over their father's bed when they entered the little room, pressing against the side of the plastic tent. He turned abruptly. Frank and Joe saw his look of surprise, followed by a slight but friendly smile.

"No change," he said, and his eyes shifted to Al. The hint of a smile vanished. "Only family is allowed in this room."

"This is our cousin, Al Garribay," Joe said,

thankful they had worked out their story ahead of time. "He flew in today to stay with Dad while we're out."

"Where are you going?" Thomas said with sudden interest.

Frank and Joe were silent for a moment.

"We're going to try to piece together Dad's last day before he came here," Joe lied.

"Of course," Thomas said, smiling. "But Mr. Garribay doesn't need to stay. I'll watch your father while you're gone. There's no need to expose anyone unnecessarily."

"But he's my uncle," Al said convincingly. "What if he regains consciousness? Someone should be here—someone he knows."

Thomas frowned and was about to object again when Frank and Joe heard their father's voice and spun around to find Fenton's eyes open for the first time since they had arrived in Borneo.

"Joe, Frank," Fenton whispered. The foursome quickly gathered around the bed, with Joe and Frank closest to Fenton's head on one side, and Thomas on the other. Al stood at the foot of the bed.

"Yes, Dad, we're here," Frank said through the plastic sheet, but Fenton's eyes slipped shut and Frank felt his hope fade again.

Then Fenton took a deep breath, as though mustering his strength. He opened his eyes and pushed himself up on one elbow, his eyes searching the four faces gathered around him. His gaze seemed to pause for an instant on Thomas, then focused on Joe and Frank.

"Get the doctor," he mumbled weakly. "He's the one."

Chapter

9

"The doctor?" Frank asked his dad urgently.

It was already too late. Fenton had once again lapsed into unconsciousness, his face deathly white, his jaw slack.

"Dad, Dad," Joe cried, but there was no response.

"I'm afraid it's no use," Thomas said, gently pulling Joe away. "He can't hear you. It's the sickness, it makes him babble. I'm sorry."

"But he was conscious," Joe said, slipping out of Thomas's grip. "And that's all the more reason for Al to stay here. Dad could wake up again."

Thomas nodded weakly and didn't object when Al sat down in the straight-backed chair at the foot of the bed. "Of course," he said, "but I'd

like a few more words with you—will you two
come to the lab?"

Joe looked back at his dad. He was tired and
wanted more than anything to stay with Fenton.
But there was nothing more he could do. They
had to keep moving if they were going to solve
this mystery. He nodded and followed Thomas
and Frank out.

"I wanted to talk in private," Thomas said
when they were in the lab. "Are you sure you
shouldn't stay here? Is your trip really so important?"

Frank studied Thomas for a minute, noting the
concern in his eyes. "Yes, it is. We're going to
look for the cure to anthrax-B. But now I'm more
worried than ever about leaving Dad. He seemed
to be referring to the doctor in there."

"Except that Dad said *he,* and Dr. Tokunaga
is a woman," Joe said, folding his arms across
his chest.

"*He* and *she* are only one letter different,"
Thomas explained sadly. "And I've had concerns
about the doctor myself. I didn't tell you before,
but she's been acting strange lately, meeting people in the night when she thinks I'm not around
and making phone calls to Pakistan. I've seen the
numbers on the phone bills. I'm simply not sure
that you can depend on her to help your father.
Where are you going to look for the cure?"

"Up the river a ways," Joe said with a wave
of his hand. "Jungle Mulvaney said there may

have been a vial filled with the cure lost there years ago."

"It's certainly a long shot," Thomas said seriously. "But I'll do everything I can to keep your father safe while you're gone."

"Thanks," Frank agreed. "But I still wish we could learn more about Dr. Tokunaga."

"Yeah, but even if we solved that mystery, it wouldn't help Dad," Joe said, shaking his head slowly. "Finding the cure has to be our top priority."

"Where is the doctor now?" Frank asked, pushing the door to the lab open. The three walked into the hall and moved toward the hospital exit.

"Out," Thomas said with a shrug. "She doesn't tell me where she's going, just when she'll be back. This time she said a couple of hours."

"Have you known her long?" Joe asked. He wondered if Dr. Tokunaga had gone off to meet with the Assassins.

"I've been here only three weeks," Thomas said, shoving his hands in the pockets of his lab coat. "I was hired after Dr. Tokunaga's last assistant died of a heart attack right here in the hospital."

"Where are you from?" Frank asked, still unable to place his accent.

"From England originally," Thomas said. "But I've been here and there around the world for so many years, it's hard to know where to call home."

"You do have an unusual accent," Frank commented. "What about Dr. Tokunaga's friends?" he went on casually. "Do you know any of them?"

Thomas shook his head and raised his eyebrows in a you've-got-to-be-kidding expression. "I've never seen the doctor with anyone except on business. I don't think she has friends, and personally, I can understand why. She's a cold fish—won't even let me call her by her first name. Acts as if she has something to hide."

The three had arrived at the front door. Now Thomas opened it for them, again promising to watch out for Fenton.

It was a short walk along a dusty road to Bidai's longhouse. Even so, they were half an hour late for their six-thirty dinner date. They passed through a banana plantation, then through the gardens around the longhouse. They were met by an escort of young boys at the edge of the Iban compound. One of the boys ran ahead, and Bidai was waiting at the top of the longhouse steps when they arrived.

The longhouse was a long shed with a thatched roof, built on stilts several feet above the ground. A few pigs and chickens roamed in the shade beneath the building.

A long log with notches hacked out of it for

steps led up from the ground to the floor of the longhouse.

Bidai watched with satisfaction as the guys easily maneuvered the rustic staircase.

"You Hardys have good balance," Bidai said when they reached the top. "You'll do all right in the jungle."

Frank and Joe were now standing on a small bamboo porch. All at once Joe saw a flash of red in the trees nearby. Bidai's smile widened.

"I have a treat for you," he said, and, signaling Frank and Joe to wait, disappeared inside the longhouse, returning with three fresh bananas.

Bidai trotted nimbly down the log ladder and headed into the jungle with Joe and Frank following him to a small clearing. Vines wrapped the tree trunks around them with leaves, and in the open space, tall grass waved in a gentle breeze.

"Be very still," Bidai said quietly, then called out, "Pegila."

The word was barely out of his mouth before a furry red ape swung to the ground and ambled up to him.

"It's an orangutan," Frank gasped. He knew the endangered species was native to Borneo but had never expected to see one.

"Pegila's an orphan," Bidai explained, handing a banana to each of them. "We will feed her until she's old enough to take care of herself."

"Most orangutans live in preserves," Bidai said

sadly, "but we have a small band here. Sometimes poachers kill the mothers and steal the babies to sell as pets. A hunter tried to steal this one, but I chased him away."

Frank and Joe looked at the young ape. She was about half the size of either brother, with sad, dark eyes and long, shaggy red hair. She took a banana from Bidai first, then carefully walked across the clearing to snatch a piece of fruit from Joe, staying as far from him as possible. After collecting the third banana from Frank, the orangutan ran for the trees. Within seconds she was gone, melding into the trees so completely that neither of the Hardys could pick her out of the foliage.

"That's a pretty exotic pet," Joe said when the orangutan was gone.

"Not a pet," Bidai said. "She's wild—mostly—and when she learns to find her own food, we won't see her much anymore. Now we'd better get back or we'll miss dinner."

They took the jungle path back to the longhouse. Following Bidai's instructions, the Hardys removed their shoes before entering the longhouse. Inside, more than a hundred people were sitting on the bamboo floor of the big building. One side of the longhouse was completely open to the jungle. The other side, nearest the river, was divided into rooms with bamboo walls. Bidai explained that the rooms were for the twenty-eight families that lived in the longhouse.

One family seemed to be set apart from the others. The man was covered with deep blue tattoos.

"This is our *Tuai Rumah*—our headman," Bidai said, directing the brothers toward him. They walked the length of the longhouse and stood in front of the *Tuai Rumah* as their guide introduced them. Then Bidai directed them to an empty space on the floor next to the head family.

As Frank settled himself, cross-legged, Bidai explained, "The headman is our chief."

Joe seated himself on the floor, then turned to Bidai. "If you don't hunt heads, what are those?" he asked, pointing to the ceiling.

Directly above them was a crude net woven from bark and filled with at least a dozen shrunken, blackened heads.

"They are very old," Bidai whispered.

"Then they're real?" Joe asked.

Bidai nodded. "My ancestors brought the heads back from wars. We keep them for good luck—and as reminders that we are stronger than our enemies."

"Remind me not to be your enemy," Joe said.

Bidai laughed. "Don't worry, Joe. I won't hang your head up there."

Joe was distracted from the heads by several women wearing colorful skirtlike sarongs who had begun to walk around the great room serving food from large platters. As they got closer, the guys began to smell an odor like rotting onions.

The women scooped big chunks of light-colored meat onto their plates, along with rice and several whitish green pieces of fruit. The guys quickly figured out that the smell was coming from the fruit.

"I'm not very hungry," Joe whispered to Bidai, who sat beside him, clearly pleased with the meal.

"It's an insult if you don't eat," Bidai said seriously. "Besides, this is the python you fought today."

Joe grimaced.

"What's this green stuff?" Frank asked.

"Durian," Bidai said with a laugh. "It's the best-tasting fruit in the world. You're lucky it's in season. Just ignore the smell."

"Right," Joe said skeptically.

Deciding to get it over with, Frank tried a small bite of the durian and quickly broke into a smile.

"Bidai's right, this stuff is great," he said. "Kind of like onion-flavored ice cream. Loosen up, Joe. Remember, you're supposed to give new foods a chance."

Joe frowned but tasted the fruit.

"Okay. It's the best stuff on earth," he said, forcing a smile. "But I'm feeling generous tonight. I'm going to let you have my share."

Bidai laughed and dug into his own plate of food.

Frank and Joe finally got through the meal, agreeing that the python and sweet potatoes were edible but bland. They were just finishing when they heard the gentle cadence of drums and looked up to see a column of warriors dressed for battle parade into the room. Their faces were painted with colored streaks. Each one carried a spear and shield decorated with hornbill feathers and designs.

Joe and Frank set their plates on the floor. As the drums grew louder and the beat quickened, the circle of warriors closed around them.

"Did Bidai say anything to you about entertainment?" Joe whispered to Frank nervously.

"Not a word," Frank answered, watching the warriors.

The drums beat louder as the circle tightened in front of the Hardys. The warriors held their spears at an angle across their bodies, beating the ends together. Every so often they lunged forward, as if to attack—sending goose bumps down Joe's spine.

Then, suddenly, the circle parted and a single warrior wearing a clouded leopard skin leaped through the opening. He landed inches from Frank and Joe with a bloodcurdling yell, holding large machetelike swords in each hand, ready to strike.

Chapter

10

THE LEAD WARRIOR raised his swords toward the ceiling so they crossed above his head, then brought them down slowly in front of him, ready to lash out with both lethal weapons at once.

Joe and Frank sat frozen in place, wondering whether they'd been right to suspect Bidai. Had the Iban been drawing them into this trap all along?

There was no way out of the circle of warriors. Joe's muscles tensed. He was ready to defend himself but didn't think he stood much chance against the Ibans' razor-sharp swords. "Any ideas," he whispered to Frank.

"None," Frank whispered back, his eyes searching the warriors for some point of weakness. Then Bidai stepped out in front of Frank and Joe, facing the sword-wielding warrior. He said some words in Iban, then turned back to the guys, a big smile on his face.

"The *Tuai Rumah* is honoring us before our trip," he said with pride. "He's planned a celebration."

Joe's fists relaxed as the leader slowly lowered his swords and bowed down in front of them. He could clearly see the soft pattern in the leopard skin draped over his shoulders. Then the warrior straightened up, touched Frank and Joe on the arm, and led them to the *Tuai Rumah.*

The old man rose and began to speak. "My son says you have an important mission."

Joe and Frank stared at each other and then at Bidai.

"He's your dad?" Joe whispered.

Bidai smiled and nodded. Suddenly the guys understood why all the Ibans at the hotel treated Bidai the way they did—he was the chief's son.

Frank swallowed hard before speaking to the headman. "We are looking for a cure for a disease that is killing my father," he said. "We think that other people will get sick from the same disease eventually. Finding a cure could protect everyone in Borneo and the world."

The *Tuai Rumah* nodded seriously. He sat absolutely straight on the low platform, his legs crossed, a bodyguard flanking him on either side. "My son says you have a map. May I see it?"

Frank looked at Joe, who tipped his chin in a

barely noticeable nod. Joe knew what his brother was thinking.

Frank slipped the map of Borneo out of his money belt and carefully unfolded it. He handed it to the *Tuai Rumah* and waited for a moment while the headman examined it.

"We want to go here," Frank said, pointing to the small *x* on the north side of the Rajang River. "A man disappeared in the jungle during the war. He was carrying the cure. That *x* marks his last known location."

The *Tuai Rumah* frowned. "The man will be gone by now," he said. "The jungle doesn't leave its dead."

"We're hoping he built a shelter or found a cave—something that might have survived," Frank said. He knew their mission sounded hopeless, but with his father's life at stake, no odds were too high to take. He tried to make his voice sound enthusiastic to cover his doubts. "The cure was in a glass vial, so it's possible it's intact."

The *Tuai Rumah*'s frown deepened and, for the first time, he looked at his son.

"This is very dangerous country," he said to Bidai. "Ukit country."

Frank wanted to ask what Ukit country was, but Bidai was already speaking.

"The Ukits can help us," Bidai said, staring his father straight in the eye. "They are the greatest hunters. They know every tree in the jungle. They will know if the man left anything behind."

"The Ukits may not want to help," the *Tuai Rumah* said gravely. "They may think you're trespassers."

"I know the language of the jungle," Bidai said after a moment. "You taught me how to make the messages yourself. The Ukits won't hurt us if they know we are friends."

The *Tuai Rumah* was silent for several moments, giving Frank and Joe time to consider what they would do if Bidai was forbidden to lead them. They couldn't go into the jungle alone, and there wasn't time to find another guide. Their mission was in jeopardy even before it started.

"It could be important to your whole tribe," Joe pleaded. "And whether we find the cure or not, we'll be back in two days." Joe swallowed hard. He didn't want to think about failure, about what would happen to his dad if he and Frank were forced to return to Kijang without the cure.

The *Tuai Rumah* sighed softly and remained silent for another minute.

"Very well," he said at last, and then turned to Frank and Joe. "Follow Bidai's instructions carefully, and don't make the mistake of thinking the Ukits are not watching. They are always watching."

Then, turning to the rest of the tribe, the *Tuai Rumah* said in a loud voice, "My son will lead the Americans into the jungle tomorrow to seek a cure for a dangerous disease. Tonight we wish them a safe journey and a speedy return."

There was a cheer from the crowd, and the somber warriors surrounding Joe, Frank, and Bidai were suddenly all smiles. They quickly formed a loose circle and, as the drums began again, started a rhythmic dance, moving around the big room.

Bidai grinned broadly as he invited Frank and Joe to join the line of dancers. They quickly picked up the steps and were soon whirling around the circle to the beat of the drums.

They danced for half an hour before Joe pulled Bidai aside. "What's so dangerous about Ukit country anyway?" he asked, speaking loudly so he could be heard over the drums.

Bidai frowned at Joe for a moment. "I'll tell you," he said. "But let's go where it's quiet."

Joe motioned to Frank, who was across the room, still dancing between two painted Iban warriors. He slipped out of the circle and followed Joe and Bidai along the open side of the longhouse.

When they were almost to the far end of the building, Bidai ducked into a small cubicle. It was quieter inside, though the guys could still hear the beat of the drums. There was a woven mat on the floor and two large carved boxes pushed against the wall. A few clothes were strewn around and a blanket was pushed to one end of the mat.

Bidai motioned to the brothers to sit on the floor.

"About the Ukits," Joe went on, finding a spot in the corner and crossing his legs.

"They live in the jungle, where that x is on the map," Bidai said seriously. "They don't live in longhouses as we do, just in the trees. They are very good hunters and strong warriors. Nobody makes trouble with the Ukits."

"But you said it would be okay," Frank asked.

"It will be," Bidai replied firmly. "Father just said those things to make us be careful."

"He made the Ukits sound like some kind of commandos," Joe commented.

"Sort of, but not the kind in your American movies," Bidai said. "The Ukits still hunt with blowpipes."

"And poison darts?" Joe asked anxiously, thinking immediately of his father.

Bidai nodded and pointed to the end of his small room, where two long branches lay against the wall. He picked one up carefully and handed it to Joe.

The branch was seven feet long and almost perfectly straight. It had been hollowed out to form a long tube with an opening through the middle about the size of a pencil.

"This is a blowpipe?" Joe asked excitedly. "I've heard you can kill a wild boar with one of these from a hundred feet away."

"That's right, and the Ukits are more accurate

than that," Bidai said. "The Iban use them mostly for fun now, but the Ukits still make poison from the sap of a tree that can kill a man in minutes."

"I've heard that in World War Two the Japanese feared blowpipes more than any modern weapon," Joe said. He handed the blowpipe to Frank, who held it up as though aiming it.

"That's right," Bidai said with pride. Then, shaking his head at Frank, he added, "But if you shoot like that, you'll hit nothing but ground. You're holding it upside down."

Frank looked confused, since the pipe was just a straight tube.

"It's crafted with a top and bottom side," Joe said. "I remember reading about it. It's made with a slight curve, so when you hold it up, the weight of the ends makes it exactly straight. But if you hold it upside down, the curve is exaggerated."

Frank looked through the tube. He turned it in his hands until he could see light from the other end.

"It would seem that Joe knows a little about the jungle," Bidai commented wryly.

"And you know a little about life in our country," Joe said. He'd caught sight of a handheld video game, mostly hidden by one of Bidai's shirts.

Bidai followed his gaze and pulled out the

game—it was the same brand Joe had back home.

"It was a gift from someone I guided for," he said. "It's a lot of fun, but the batteries are dead now. Besides, it's hard to get games here. I only have one, and it's getting pretty old."

Joe looked at the game for a moment. It seemed out of place, but he remembered that while Bidai danced with painted warriors and lived in a longhouse, he also drove a car and spoke English. Life in Borneo was a mixture of the old and the new.

"Tomorrow when we head into the jungle, will we be going in a dugout canoe or a speedboat?" Joe asked, grinning.

"Both," Bidai said. "We'll go in a dugout canoe with a motor."

"What do we need to take?" Frank said.

"Just a change of clothes," Bidai replied as he stood up. "We'll leave at dawn."

It was well after 11:00 P.M. when the Hardys returned to the White Hornbill Hotel. Bidai had let them take his battered green car so they wouldn't be late in the morning. Joe had been especially pleased by this since it meant he could use the car to follow their midnight caller from the hotel.

Inghai, the desk clerk, was waiting for them when they entered the lobby.

"How was dinner?" he asked, smiling warmly.

Frank and Joe realized that the hotel staff had been forced to miss the celebration because of their work.

"Great," Joe answered, chuckling. "I think the durians are an acquired taste."

Joe asked Inghai for an envelope and a piece of paper. He folded the blank paper and slid it into the envelope, then sealed the flap.

"Give this to our friend," he said, handing the envelope back to the clerk.

They went over the signal again. Then Joe left the hotel to hide in Bidai's car in the alley across the street.

Frank went upstairs and settled beside the balustrade along the landing of the second floor to wait for Inghai's signal.

It was eleven-thirty when the desk clerk moved the pen set to the opposite side of the registration book. He did it casually as a dark man in a trench coat and hat walked into the lobby.

Frank went quickly to the room, closed the door behind him, stood at the window, and peered out. The front of Bidai's car was barely visible in the dim light of a lone street lamp. But instead of seeing the silhouette of his brother sitting behind the wheel, Frank saw that the door on the passenger side was open. The car was empty, and among the shadows of the alley he saw the dark shape of a body lying on the cobblestones.

Chapter

11

"Joe," Frank whispered, then bolted down the stairs and out the front door of the hotel. As he dashed across the street, Frank saw the man in the trench coat slip around the corner. He didn't care because he was focused only on helping Joe.

He knelt beside his brother and touched his neck, finding a pulse. "Joe!" he cried, shaking him gently.

Joe groaned and sat up slowly, rubbing the back of his head. "Our man got away?"

"Yeah," Frank said. "What happened?"

"I guess I was spotted," Joe said. "I was waiting in the car just as we planned, but about eleven-thirty, I heard someone behind me. Before I could turn around, I got hit over the head. There must have been two of them because I heard them talking just before I blacked out completely. One said, 'Tell Medicine Man the coast is clear.' ''

"That could be the doctor," Frank said.

"Yeah, except that she's a woman," Joe replied.

"Still, if Medicine Man's a code name, it could refer to a woman," Frank commented, getting slowly to his feet and then helping his brother up. "Did you hear anything else?"

"Something about calling the chief in Islamabad," Joe added, suddenly excited. "That's the capital of Pakistan."

"How'd you know that?" Frank knew that Joe was better at football than geography.

"I remember it from Marsha Bailey's report in social studies. I also remember seeing a Pakistani rupee on Dr. Tokunaga's desk the day we were in her office. The Gray Man said the lab where the Assassins are developing their germ weapons is in Pakistan."

"You're right," Frank said, raising an eyebrow. "It sounds to me like Tokunaga could be working for the Assassins."

"If we had another day, I bet we could prove it," Joe said, walking around Bidai's car to retrieve the keys from the ignition. "Maybe we should stay here and try."

"But if we catch her now, Dad will still die," Frank reminded him. "We need a cure, and the

Assassins don't have that. If they did, they wouldn't be bugging us."

"It's going to be hard to leave Dad with her," Joe said.

"Yeah, but we have to trust Al and the Gray Man," Frank said. "We'll stop by the hospital tomorrow to tell Al what's happening. We can see Dad once more, too."

Joe couldn't say anything. He didn't want to think about saying goodbye to his father.

It was 6:30 A.M. and still dark when Joe and Frank climbed out of their beds, dressed, and headed for the hospital. The streets were deserted, and inside the building a maid was sweeping the hallway when Joe pushed the front door open. She smiled as they passed, and the hardwood floor creaked under their feet. Al was on his feet the minute the boys turned the knob to the door of Fenton's room.

There had been little change in their father's condition, Al said, but once during the night Fenton had started thrashing around in his bed.

"Convulsions?" Joe asked anxiously, remembering that was the last stage of anthrax.

"No," Al said reassuringly.

The Hardys told Al about the attack on Joe the night before. By now the Assassins would know that the envelope they'd left at the front desk contained only a blank piece of paper, meaning they might try to fulfill their promise to kill Fenton.

Before leaving, Frank and Joe turned back to their dad. Frank wanted to touch him but couldn't because of the plastic tent.

"Hang on, Dad," Joe said from beside him. "We'll be back." Joe put his hand on Frank's shoulder and jerked his head toward the door.

"Do you think he heard you?" Frank asked when they were in the hall.

"Yeah." Joe nodded, managing a smile.

The guys were about to leave the hospital when Joe touched Frank's arm and pointed to the door of Dr. Tokunaga's office. It was partway open, though the inside was dark. Frank knew immediately what his brother had in mind.

Joe crossed the corridor and pushed the door open. Then both boys stepped in. Frank closed the door behind him as Joe found the light switch. The office was as orderly as ever, the big wooden desk completely clear of clutter.

"What are we looking for?" Frank asked as they surveyed the room.

"Anything connecting the doctor with the Assassins," Joe said, walking to the file cabinet. "Or with research in Pakistan."

While Joe poked through the files, Frank checked out the desk. In the center drawer he found the doctor's day planner and flipped through the tabs. Behind one labeled Top Priority Frank found a small piece of yellow notepaper clipped to the page. On it was a phone number, complete with a country code he didn't recognize.

Frank reached for the phone and dialed.

"Got something?" Joe asked, turning away from his files.

"Maybe," Frank said.

A man answered after the second ring.

"Pakistan National Hospital," the voice said.

As he listened, Frank saw the doorknob turn.

"Company," he whispered, quickly replacing the receiver. He slipped the planner back in the desk and pushed the drawer shut just as the office door opened.

Joe had pushed the drawer to the file cabinet shut and was leaning lazily against the wall when Dr. Tokunaga walked in. Her look of surprise turned quickly to one of anger.

"What are you doing here?" she demanded, clenching the knob hard.

"I was just making a call," Frank offered. Then, thinking quickly, he added, "Thomas said we could use your phone anytime."

Dr. Tokunaga's face became dark with rage, and she slammed the office door behind her. "That insubordinate loafer," she growled. "My luck ran out the day he showed up."

Frank and Joe exchanged looks.

"I thought you needed him to fill a vacancy," Joe said, trying to draw the doctor out.

"I did," Dr. Tokunaga said, her voice a little softer. She sighed and moved toward her high-backed desk chair. "My last assistant and I worked together for five years. He never ran tests I didn't order or took time off without asking— like Thomas does."

Dr. Tokunaga sat down in her chair and stared straight ahead, focusing in the distance. Frank guessed she was remembering her former assistant.

"How did he die?" Frank asked gently.

Dr. Tokunaga shook her head. "One day he just walked into my office—something he never did without knocking. His mouth was open as if he was going to say something, but instead he simply dropped dead. It was a heart attack. I tried to save him but couldn't."

Dr. Tokunaga paused, then went on. "Three days later Thomas Wilson walked in looking for work," she said frowning. "His background was perfect, and he had good letters of reference from two hospitals in Pakistan. I couldn't believe my luck. I tried to check his references, but both the doctors he listed were out of town. I was so swamped with work I hired him anyway. Now I'm sorry I ever met him. He disobeys my orders, his work is sloppy, and he lets strangers into my office. In fact, I'm getting ready to call the Pakistani hospitals again to check his references."

Thomas's arrival in Kijang right after the death of Dr. Tokunaga's first assistant struck Joe as a bizarre coincidence. Could the assistant have been killed to make a position for Thomas? If so, did that mean Thomas was the Assassin—and not Dr. Tokunaga?

"Who else did Thomas let into your office?" Joe asked, sitting in a chair opposite her desk.

"Someone from out of town," Dr. Tokunaga said. "I walked in early, just like today, and Thomas and this man were going through our records. In fact, they had your father's file out."

"Was that before we arrived in Borneo?" Frank asked suspiciously.

"Same day, I think," Dr. Tokunaga said. "Thomas said the man was from mainland Malaysia checking records for the government, but he left two Pakistani rupees on my desk. Thomas has lied before, so I don't really trust him."

"Lied about what?" Joe asked with interest.

"He called in sick one day, but our delivery man saw him meeting someone at the airport."

Frank remembered the first time they'd met Thomas. He'd been gruff until Joe mentioned Fenton's name, but friendly ever since. And yesterday he'd seemed especially interested in where they were going. Frank suddenly regretted having told him.

"When we visited Jungle Mulvaney he told us you'd been there, too," Frank said, watching her eyes.

The doctor seemed to be startled and angry for a moment. She calmed herself by sucking in a long breath of air. "I knew about the Japanese killing people with anthrax-B during the war," she said. "And I knew your father's symptoms were similar, but I didn't want the word getting out that anthrax-B was back. The Japanese would be blamed again. I went to Jungle Mulvaney to be sure I wasn't overlooking a cure. If he'd given me any hope of finding something to help your father, I would have started a search for it. But he didn't. Believe me, I've done everything possible to help him."

Joe found himself believing her and fearing they'd made a grave mistake by trusting Thomas. Leaving their father now was going to be harder than ever. But the cure could still be someplace in the Borneo jungle, and they had to find it or Fenton Hardy was a dead man. They would have to trust Al to handle the Assassin, whoever he—or she—was. He tapped his watch, reminding Frank they were late for their rendezvous with Bidai.

Frank nodded. They left Dr. Tokunaga at her desk, a frown creasing her forehead, and hurried out of the building to Bidai's car.

"You drive just like Bidai," Frank complained as Joe steered them down the cobblestone street at breakneck speed.

"It's the car," Joe said lightly. "This is the only speed it goes. Besides, we don't want to miss our boat."

"I know, but I wish we'd had time to talk to Al again," Frank said as the trunks of banana palms flashed by the speeding car. "I'm not so sure Dr. Tokunaga is the Assassin anymore. Thomas could be 'Medicine Man.' He seems to have connections in Pakistan and he, or the stranger he was with, could have left the rupees on the doctor's desk. If Dr. Tokunaga is telling the truth, they were going through Dad's records. Plus, Thomas was the last one in the lab before it was ransacked. Maybe he had let the intruder in. The Assassins could have killed Dr. Tokunaga's assistant to make an opening for Thomas.

"Yeah, or Dr. Tokunaga could be lying," Joe reminded him. "And I'm still not sure I believe her story about the reason she went to Jungle Mulvaney's. She could really have been trying to find the map. When she learned Mulvaney had given it to Dad, maybe she guessed that he sent it to us."

"Well, we'll just have to rely on Al to take care of Medicine Man. We've got to concentrate on finding the cure," Frank said as Joe turned in at the drive to the Iban longhouse, stopping by a short wooden dock on the Rajang River. Bidai and a group of other Ibans were waiting beside a dugout canoe, already packed with supplies.

"I thought you'd stolen my car and left town," Bidai scolded. "The sun has been up for half an hour."

"Sorry," Joe said. "We had to make a stop at the hospital."

"How's your father?" Bidai asked, helping them put their small bags in the canoe.

"The same, maybe worse," Joe said, stepping into the bow of the boat.

Bidai directed Frank to sit in the middle, then started the outboard motor and guided the boat quickly into the main current of the greenish river. Iban boys and girls waved to them from the shore.

Soon the jungle closed in around them. Bidai steered the canoe around boulders and floating logs with the same reckless style he used when driving a car. This time, though, the guys didn't complain. They were desperate to get to their destination to look for the cure before it was too late.

They stopped for lunch along a quiet sandbar just above a long stretch of barren land where loggers had stripped away the trees. Bidai sadly told them how loggers had destroyed much of the jungle and were cutting down more every day.

Several times they came to short but dangerous rapids where the water rushed over rocks too swiftly for the outboard motor to power through. The shore was so matted with foliage that they couldn't carry the canoe around these spots. Instead, Bidai steered the boat as close to the shore as possible and the three of them got out and hauled it up and over the rocks, fighting the current as they went. At the top of each rapids, they collapsed back in the canoe and let the boat carry them along the next stretch of calm water.

They approached the steepest rapids of all just as the sun had begun to dip behind the horizon. Bidai stopped the boat. By the bank on their right, the water dropped four feet over a pair of huge boulders. A third boulder divided the river in two parts. To the left of it was a narrow strip of rapids. At the bottom of the big drop on the right was a powerful whirlpool where the two channels converged.

"I'm not sure we can make this one," Bidai said.

"We have to," Joe yelled over the sound of rushing water. He jumped out and started to pull the canoe toward the rapids on the left.

Bidai and Frank followed his lead and took their positions for the scramble up the watery incline. Bidai walked at the front of the canoe. Frank was on the left nearest the bank, and Joe took the right side. The water beat at their knees as they pushed the canoe up the rocky grade one step at a time, feeling for footholds under the torrent.

They were nearly at the top, and Joe could see the swirling whirlpool below when he heard Bidai yell. He looked around in time to see their guide stumble and fall. The water quickly pulled him away from the canoe and down the rapids. Joe reached out and Bidai grabbed for him. Their hands touched, but the young Iban was swept past the big boulder that divided the river toward the whirlpool below.

"Help!" Bidai called as he circled twice in the green swirl. Then he was sucked under the foaming water.

Chapter

12

JOE WATCHED, horrified, as the water swallowed Bidai. He knew the whirlpool was too strong for any swimmer to escape. There was only one way to save their guide.

Joe turned away from the canoe, leaving Frank to wrestle it as close to shore as he could. He scrambled to the boulder that divided the river, pulled himself up, and stood right over the dark whirlpool below.

Joe took a deep breath and dove into the water, pushing off hard from the rock. He hit the water on the edge of the whirlpool, and his body shot through the current like a missile. As he passed through the heart of the whirlpool, his left arm found Bidai. Joe's momentum was just strong enough to pull them both from the center of the whirlpool. Then Joe kicked furiously and managed to reach the outer edges of the watery trap with Bidai in tow.

They reached the still water near the riverbank, and Bidai popped to the surface, gasping for air. Joe had to help him to shore, where they both collapsed, coughing and choking.

On the opposite bank, Frank had caught an overhanging branch and pulled himself onto it, dragging the canoe behind. He was still clutching the boat but tiring. If he let it go, their only transportation would be shattered on the rocks right below him. He had to ease it back down to the calm waters at the bottom of the rapids.

Carefully, he clambered back into the river and guided the boat downstream while the dark water rushed against the canoe, tugging at the bow.

Frank hung on, his arms aching. He was almost to the bottom of the rapids and near a still pool protected by a circle of rocks. He stepped over the rocks, pulling the canoe with him, but his right foot sank into the mud and onto the back of a large monitor lizard hiding there.

With a flick of its tail, the lizard was gone, throwing Frank's feet out from under him. He fell backward just as a rush of water caught the canoe and pulled it into the rapids.

Frank jumped to his feet and leaped for the canoe, catching the gunwale with his fingertips. He got his footing again and dragged the boat to shore. Exhausted, he could only wave weakly to

Joe and Bidai, who had been watching from the other side. Joe erupted into a series of cheers when Frank finally got the canoe to safety.

"I am shamed," Bidai said when he finally got to his feet. "I've been saved in the jungle by Americans."

Joe turned to see that Bidai was grinning. "I guess we paid you back for saving us from the python," Joe said, patting the young Iban on the shoulder. "Now let's get back across this river."

Bidai led the way downstream to a place where the river widened and was calmer.

"Do you have piranhas in Borneo?" Joe asked as they prepared to swim across the river.

"No, just a few crocs," Bidai called over his shoulder as he waded in. "But don't worry, we're safe here—I think."

When Bidai was waist deep in the murky water, he did an expert surface dive and came up swimming smoothly, reaching the far bank in a dozen or so powerful strokes.

Joe was right behind him, and after they made their way to where Frank was still holding the canoe, they prepared to attack the river once again.

"No breaks for swimming this time," Joe told Bidai teasingly.

"Agreed," the guide said, wearing his customary lighthearted smile. As they started up the river once more, Bidai's expression became serious. He had to concentrate hard on the slippery rocks and bubbling water. Joe and Frank walked behind him, hauling the boat between them.

When they reached the top, Bidai halted. "We can make camp here," he said, surveying a sand-bar in front of them and the jungle beyond. The sun had almost completely disappeared below the horizon.

Bidai chose a spot fifty yards back from the river where three teak trees grew in a triangle. He supplied Joe and Frank with long knives from the bundles in the canoe and showed them how to cut poles. It took him just a few minutes to bind three poles crosswise between the trees, forming the framework for the floor of their shelter four feet above the ground. Then he started to stack other poles across the bottom as flooring.

"Why don't we just sleep on the ground?" Joe asked. "It would be a lot easier."

"Yes, but you never know when the rain will come," Bidai said. "The river can rise several feet in an hour or two. It is no fun to wake up in the night swimming."

Bidai showed them how to make a sloping roof over their platform out of crisscrossed branches. While they finished that job, he disappeared into the jungle and came back with a huge pile of palm leaves, which he used to thatch the roof.

"I guess we'll be safe from everything in there," Joe commented, surveying the little hut.

"Not yet," Bidai said, and disappeared into the jungle again. He returned with a bowl-like leaf full of sap. Using a stick he spread the sap in bands around the trunk of each teak tree, halfway between the ground and their shelter.

"That will keep the ants away," he said, finally satisfied with his work.

"Ants?" Joe asked, wrinkling his nose.

"Yes," Bidai said casually. "Man-eating ants. They come in the night, and by morning there's nothing left but bones. But don't worry. They can't cross this sticky barrier."

Joe's eyes widened, and he took a walk around to make sure Bidai hadn't missed any spots.

The construction project had taken less time than Joe and Frank might have spent pitching a tent back home, and they still had time for a cold dinner before darkness completely engulfed them.

They were finishing up their smoked fish and rice when Frank pulled the map from his money belt. "Where are we now?" he asked.

Bidai studied the map. "This is the falls we just came up," he said, pointing to a spot on the river not far from their destination. "Tomorrow we will walk into the jungle for about five miles to find the place on the map."

Joe felt a wave of excitement. Everything depended on what happened the next day.

Frank was refolding the map when an odd, moist breeze blew through camp and the jungle became oddly quiet. Joe and Frank went on instant alert, thinking that the silence of the jungle animals might signal some human intruder. Bidai's concern was different.

"Rain," he said, jumping to his feet.

He ran the half-dozen steps to the canoe and dragged it up the sandbar as far from the river as he could. Then he and Frank tied both ends high up on the trunks of two meranti trees so that a flood would not take it away. Joe hung their supplies in waterproof bags from a branch.

By the time they finished, huge drops of water had started to fall, splattering off the river rocks and sending them running for shelter.

Inside, they looked out on the darkened world as rain pounded on the leaves high above. Suddenly lightning flashed across the night sky, and a fierce wind began to howl through the trees so that the branches swayed and rattled. Frank agreed to take the first watch, and Joe and Bidai fell asleep listening to the rain and thunder.

The rain had stopped by the time Bidai woke Joe for the last watch of the night. Joe lay under the thatched roof for more than an hour, listening to the cadence of cicada and croaking frogs, but seeing nothing. Then, just before dawn, something moved by the river. He raised up on his elbows and peered between the poles that formed the walls of their shelter.

In the dimness he could just make out two men dressed in military camouflage, working at the ropes on their canoe. Both had knives and cut the lines easily. Then they started to drag the boat toward the river. As they worked, several other men also dressed in camouflage walked onto the sandbar. Each one carried a semiautomatic rifle, and they were less than fifty yards away.

Chapter

13

ASSASSINS!

The word echoed silently through Joe's brain. He watched as the two men edged the boat back toward the river. The main channel of the river had risen about a foot in the night, and the current was strong. In seconds the little vessel disappeared behind the rocks in a spray of water.

The Assassins then turned toward the jungle and started to survey their surroundings, weapons ready. It was only a matter of moments before they would be discovered, Joe knew.

Joe shook Frank and Bidai awake.

"How did they know we'd be here?" Frank asked, peering out toward the river.

Joe studied Bidai. The Iban had seen the map

and could have tipped someone off about their location. Bidai's face was unreadable.

Joe quickly stifled his doubts as the Assassins started to comb the trees on either side of the sandbar.

Fortunately, the rain had washed out all of their tracks from the night before. Frank motioned to the others and moved quickly to the back of the shelter, where he silently jumped to the ground and hid behind one of the giant tree trunks.

Bidai and Joe followed, and Joe was about to lead the way into the jungle when Frank motioned toward the packs that were still hanging in the tree nearby. Joe rolled his eyes. He knew they needed their supplies and equipment, but getting them down with the Assassins so close would be dangerous.

They inched their way toward the bundles as the Assassins searched the bushes near the bank.

Joe borrowed Bidai's knife and, while the other two stayed in the cover of a huge fern, stepped into the open to retrieve their packs. He moved carefully, trying not to attract attention.

The Assassins were still searching the bushes to his left when he reached up and cut the rope that held the packs. There was a soft *twang* as the branch rebounded.

The nearest Assassin turned toward the noise and dropped into a combat-ready crouch, his gun in front of him.

Joe knew it was too late to hide. He'd been spotted.

"Run for it," Frank yelled.

In an instant he, Joe, and Bidai all dashed into the trees. They heard automatic weapons fire behind them as the Assassins sprayed the jungle, but the thick foliage had already swallowed them up and the Assassins were shooting blind.

Bidai took the lead, with Frank and Joe following at a dead run. They leaped over fallen trees and ducked under branches, moving almost as quietly as wild animals.

They could hear the Assassins thrashing through the vegetation behind them, hacking a path with machetes. For a while it seemed they would outrun their pursuers. Then the undergrowth got thicker and even Bidai was slowed by it. The sound of the Assassins' slashing grew closer. Then they found themselves surrounded by a huge patch of thorny brush too thick to push through.

Joe and Frank looked around helplessly. Just as Joe was wondering if this had been Bidai's plan all along—to lead them into an impossible spot and then leave them to the Assassins—Bidai motioned for them to follow him. He crouched down low to the ground and slipped into the wall of thorns.

Joe and Frank hesitated but saw that Bidai had completely disappeared in the thick brambles. Their only chance was to follow him. With inch-long thorns grabbing at their skin and clothes, they climbed into the thorny thicket. They fought through about two feet of the bushes before spotting Bidai, sitting in a compact ball. They imitated him, each finding a spot in the midst of the branches to sit huddled in a ball, trying to ignore the pain of hundreds of needlelike thorns piercing them.

Joe and Frank held their breath as the sound of footsteps approached, then stopped. They knew the Assassins were not more than three feet from them, trying to find their trail at the edge of the thorn bushes. There were muffled words from the Assassins as the leader gave instructions, then crashing noises as they searched to the left and right of their hiding place.

Joe felt sweat rolling down his face, and Frank fought to control his breathing. The run through the jungle had left them all winded, but now they had to breathe slowly and evenly so as not to attract attention.

They sat motionless for ten minutes, their muscles starting to cramp. Toward the end of that time the Assassins had become motionless, listening. But all was quiet, except for the buzzing of insects and the occasional call of a parrot. Finally the Assassins moved away.

The boys waited several more minutes before climbing out of the bushes. The jungle was silent around them, and there was no sign of the Assassins.

"The bushes were a great idea," Joe said, pulling a thorn from his arm. "But next time I'd prefer a different kind. That was like climbing into a bed of cactus."

Frank, too, was examining his arms and legs for stickers.

"I picked these on purpose," Bidai said, smiling wryly. "No one likes to come into a thorn bush to look for you."

"I've got to admit it worked," Joe said, frowning at an especially long thorn lodged in his arm. He was thinking that Bidai had again saved their lives and reminded himself to stop suspecting their guide.

"It may not have done us much good to escape the Assassins," Frank said angrily. "Now we're lost in the jungle with no equipment."

"I hope you're not blaming me," Bidai said.

"You could have told the Assassins where we were going," Joe said, studying Bidai's face. "You did see the map."

"But I didn't," Bidai said in a steady voice.

"I believe him," Frank said confidently. "He saved us by leading the way into that thorn bush. He didn't have to do that. And it's the second time he's come to our rescue. I would have been crushed by that python without him."

"All right," Joe said after a moment's hesitation. "But what do we do now?"

"Find the cure," Bidai said quietly. "You have a map, and the jungle will give us everything else we need."

"Let's get away from here in case the Assassins come back," Frank suggested. "Then let's find a stream. I really need a drink of water."

Bidai nodded as he examined the ground, searching among the trees. After several minutes he announced that the Assassins had gone north and led the way to the south around the thorny thicket. When he stopped again, they were standing in the midst of a clump of incredibly tall trees—some as high as a twenty-story building.

"We'll stop here for a drink," he said, reaching for one of the thick vines that hung from the trees. He slashed the vine in two with his knife and gulped down the clear water that rushed out. Then he cut vines for Joe and Frank. The water was pure and there was plenty of it, so they felt refreshed when they sat down to plan their next move.

Frank pulled the map from his money belt, congratulating himself again for keeping it there instead of with their other supplies. This was the second time he had kept the map safe from the Assassins.

He spread it out in front of them and, with Bidai's help, pinpointed their location. They were within a couple of miles of where Whitefeather had sent up his flare.

Bidai immediately cut a tree branch and carefully peeled back the bark to form white curls all around the shaft. Then he fastened it to a second branch stuck into the ground.

"What's that for?" Frank asked, returning his map to its pouch.

"It tells the Ukits we've come in peace. The three curls mean there are three of us," Bidai said, getting up to leave. "With luck, the Ukit warrior who guards this territory will come talk to us, and we can ask for his help."

Joe thought of the Ukits' lethal blowpipes and felt his skin crawl.

"What if he doesn't believe we're friendly?" Frank asked, rubbing his neck.

"They'll believe us," Bidai said confidently. "It's not the Ukits you need to worry about."

"There's something else?" Joe asked, as Bidai surveyed the tree branches above them.

"Snakes, mostly," Bidai said casually. "Not pythons this time—besides, we can kill them if we have to. But the cobras and coral snakes are very poisonous. One bite and you're dead." He slapped the back of his right hand against his left palm, making it look like a body falling to the ground.

"That's nice to know," Joe offered as Bidai turned and headed deeper into the jungle. "I was afraid we were going to get bored."

Joe and Frank were about to follow him when they heard the sound of something crashing through the bushes up ahead. Then Bidai came bounding back toward them.

"Better hurry," he yelled as he passed them and kept running.

Suddenly Joe and Frank saw a wild boar crashing through the bushes behind Bidai. The animal had a long snout and two huge tusks that stuck out from its upper jaw, pulling the sides of its mouth up in an evil grin. It was so close that the guys could smell its foul odor.

Joe and Frank headed after Bidai in another mad dash through the jungle.

"I hope we don't have to hide in the thorns again," Joe yelled.

"Yeah, but even the thorns would be better than being caught by that giant garbage disposal," Frank called back.

Then, just as quickly as it had started, the crashing behind them stopped. They turned back to see the boar standing still, shaking his head angrily but no longer charging.

"Let's pick a different route," Joe offered as Bidai slowed to a walk. "I don't like the welcoming committee on that one."

"Agreed," Bidai said. "But first, I'll leave another message."

Joe and Frank sat down to rest while Bidai made another shredded branch and stuck it in the ground in a small clearing.

They had nearly dozed off when they heard a sharp metallic click. Reflexively, both Frank and Joe jumped to their feet, but they were too late.

At the opposite edge of the clearing stood a pair of Assassins, their semiautomatic weapons trained on Joe, Frank, and Bidai.

Chapter

14

Two more Assassins emerged from the trees to their left, then four crashed through the brush on their right. Joe and Frank were still thinking of running when they heard the sound of a branch breaking behind them. They turned to see a tall man with broad shoulders and a wicked grin. He was holding a semiautomatic in front of him and seemed eager to pull the trigger.

"No sudden moves," Frank said to Bidai as the Iban got up from planting his second peeled-bark message in the ground. "Those snakes you were worried about just arrived."

"You have something of ours," one of the Assassins said, stepping toward Frank and Joe. He was the smallest of the group, with dark hair and an air of authority.

"What's that?" Joe asked, raising his chin.

"The map," the Assassin leader said. "We know you have it, so don't pretend otherwise."

"When did it become yours?" Frank asked. He knew they wouldn't be able to keep the map from the Assassins, but he didn't like the idea of handing it over, and his anger made him defiant.

"When we surrounded you," the Assassin leader said, laughing slyly. "And this time you won't escape. Now, hand over the map."

Frank didn't move.

"Buzz," the Assassin leader barked toward the two men who had first appeared. He jerked his head toward Joe and Frank. One of the gunmen handed his submachine gun to the other and crossed the clearing to frisk Frank and Joe. It took him seconds to find the money belt under Frank's shirt. He unzipped it, pulled out the map, and handed it to his superior.

The Assassin leader frowned when he unfolded it. "Where's the original?" he demanded. "I know it was sent to you."

Frank frowned, wondering how the Assassins knew so much. He decided to try to find out.

"So you were the one who broke into our house in Bayport," he said, watching the Assassin leader closely.

"That's right," the dark man said with a laugh. "And I gave you a good knock in that alley when you first arrived. I thought the map would be

124

in your luggage. I guess you were smarter than we thought."

"Smart enough not to be blackmailed," Joe said. He, too, was fishing for information.

The Assassin's face became angry. "You would have been better off if you had given me the map then," he growled. "It would have saved us all a lot of trouble. But you still haven't told me where you put the original."

"I'll tell you if you'll answer a couple of questions," Frank said. "Like how you knew my dad sent us the map."

"He told us," the Assassin said with a wicked smile. "He kept going in and out of consciousness and talking—once he even warned the two of you to guard the map."

"How did you know that?" Frank pressed.

"We have our sources." The Assassin laughed. "Now, where is the original map?"

"We left it at the hotel," Frank said with a shrug. If the Assassins didn't already know the Network was on the case, he wasn't going to tell them.

"It doesn't matter anyway," the leader growled, turning to another of his men. "Radio Medicine Man. Say we have the map. Then let's get out of here." The Assassin called Buzz tied the boys' hands in front of them and looped them all together with one long rope, then led them into the jungle. As they left the clearing, Buzz pulled up the stake Bidai had so carefully shredded.

"What's this?" he demanded, glaring at Bidai coldly.

"It's some kind of an Iban thing," Joe said before Bidai could speak. "For good luck."

"Guess it didn't work." Buzz sneered and tossed the stake onto the ground.

The guys walked in the middle of the line of Assassins for almost an hour before the leader ordered his men to make camp at the edge of a group of hardwood trees. Frank, Joe, and Bidai were tied to the trunk of one of the trees and left alone.

"Do you suppose Medicine Man will show up," Joe whispered. "I sure would like to know who it is."

"Yeah, but I'd like to get out of here more," Frank replied. He'd been trying to free himself, but his ropes held fast.

"Good plan," Joe agreed. "Any ideas on how we're going to do it?"

Frank shook his head—their situation wasn't good. Not only had they been captured by the Assassins but their map had been stolen, their equipment was gone, and time was almost up for Fenton. Desperation filled him.

"Don't make a sound," Bidai whispered.

For a moment neither Joe or Frank knew what was up. Then they spotted a small man dressed only in a loincloth and carrying a knife. He slipped out of some bushes and was moving toward them.

"Don't even twitch." Bidai ordered. "He's a Ukit."

Frank watched the man out of the corner of his eye. The newcomer was shorter than Bidai and had light skin, dark hair, and a lean, muscular body. He moved without making a sound. When he got to the tree where they were tied, he carefully cut all their ropes and then disappeared into the trees again.

"Don't move," Bidai said. "He has a plan. Ukits always do."

Joe took a deep breath and tried to calm his jangled nerves. It was hard to remain motionless, pretending that he was still tied up, when his muscles screamed to move. More than anything, though, he wanted to jump up and run for it.

Then, without warning, one of the Assassins slapped his neck as though killing a bug. A moment later he slumped to the ground in a heap.

Two other Assassins ran to their fallen comrade. One of them quickly jumped up, holding a small dart in his hand.

"He's dead," the Assassin yelled. "Blowguns!"

The words caused instant panic in the clearing, but before the Assassins could decide which way to run, two more had been hit. They grabbed at the darts in their necks before slumping to the ground.

Assassins were running for cover, grabbing at

their weapons. Then the wiry Ukit dashed through the clearing, carrying a blowpipe that was at least a foot taller than he was.

"Get him!" the leader ordered, and in an instant all the Assassins were crashing clumsily through the trees after the lone Ukit.

"He's very good," Bidai said cheerfully as he jumped up and shook off his ropes. "He let them see him on purpose."

"He saved our skins," Frank said, loosening a stubborn twist of rope from his arm. "Any idea why?"

"Let's go ask him," Bidai said urgently. "He may need our help now."

Joe nodded and then led the threesome into the jungle after the Assassins. They wove and dodged through the trees, as though they were tacklers and blockers on a football field. He could hear the Assassins ahead and wondered how they would fight armed men once they caught up. Then, suddenly, the crashing stopped.

Joe came to a halt, raising his hand to stop the others. They listened for a moment and then advanced slowly through the now quiet jungle.

As he stepped around the trunk of a large tree, Joe spotted the six surviving Assassins, standing in a semicircle on open ground among ancient sandalwood, teak, and tualang trees. Two of the Assassins had their guns at the ready. The others were bare-handed.

Across from them stood the Ukit, his blowpipe in one hand, a knife in the other—clearly no match for the Assassins.

"What should we do?" Joe whispered, crouching in the bushes. "We can't let them kill him."

Frank studied the situation. They could attack, but they'd be cut down by the Assassins' guns.

"Let's try a diversion," he suggested.

Joe frowned but agreed. He stood up, planning to make some noise to give the Ukit a chance to escape, but before he could open his mouth, the Ukit gave a bloodcurdling cry and dashed into the jungle.

The Assassins fired instantly, spraying the trees with bullets as they had done that morning at the river. This time it was different. The Assassins weren't firing blindly—they knew exactly where their target was. The Ukit had a one-in-a-million chance of coming out alive.

Chapter

15

FRANK AND JOE watched in horror as the Assassins' bullets hammered through the dense foliage. The Ukit was a dead man.

Then, while the Assassins were still firing, a shape darted out of the trees behind and to the left of the Assassins. Frank and Joe saw immediately that it was the Ukit. He had somehow escaped the gunfire and circled the clearing.

Before anyone could react, the Ukit jumped on the back of the nearest Assassin and knocked him out.

Joe dashed out from the bushes, hitting the other armed Assassin with a high karate kick just as the gunman was turning to fire on the Ukit. The gunman dropped his weapon. Before he could pick it up, Joe kicked him again and he toppled over, groggy from the blows.

Bidai and Frank were also in the clearing now, standing shoulder to shoulder with Joe and the Ukit as they faced the four remaining Assassins.

"Get them," the Assassin leader cried, and in unison the camouflaged men lunged toward the boys.

Frank caught the first one with a low kick to the ribs, throwing him off balance. Then he followed up with a roundhouse kick to the man's left cheek, sending him down like a rock.

Joe dodged a punch aimed at his jaw by a short, sturdy Assassin. The blow glanced off Joe's shoulder, and he responded with a combination right jab and left hook that knocked his attacker flat.

The two other Assassins hesitated as Bidai and the Ukit drew their knives. The Assassins knew they were outclassed. Their leader waved his hand toward the underbrush, and the two Assassins who had run headlong into Joe and Frank staggered to their feet to join the retreat.

Bidai gave a triumphant whoop, and the Ukit leaped into the air, his long black hair flying.

Neither Frank nor Joe joined their celebration.

"It's gone, isn't it?" Joe said to his brother.

Frank nodded. "The leader has it."

Bidai was suddenly serious. He had forgotten how important the map was to Frank and Joe.

Frank tried to shake off his disappointment long enough to thank the Ukit for his help.

"Tell this guy we appreciate his help," Frank said to Bidai. "He saved our lives."

Their rescuer stood with his feet slightly apart, the lean muscles of his bare chest and legs gleaming. Bidai turned to the jungle fighter and spoke slowly in a strange language, pointing to Joe and Frank as he spoke. Then the Ukit talked to Bidai and finished by turning to Joe and Frank.

"You are welcome," he said in slow but understandable English. "Thank you, also."

"His name is Isat Tamabo," Bidai said, gesturing to the Ukit. "He learned a little English from missionary teachers. He read the messages I left saying we came in peace, and he watched us. He didn't like the Assassins and their guns and wanted to make them leave Ukit territory."

Frank gave Bidai a big smile. "You were right about the messages and the Ukit," he said.

Frank and Joe were still far from relieved. Even with Isat's help they'd never find the vial without the map.

"Why are you not happy?" Isat asked through Bidai, seeing Joe's frown. "You are safe now."

"Yeah, but our father isn't," Frank explained. Slowly he told Isat the story of the World War II illness and the lost vial that held the cure. Sometimes Isat would shake his head, showing that he did not understand Frank's words. Then Bidai would explain in Isat's language.

"My father tells a story about the great war," Bidai translated for Isat when Frank finished.

"The Japanese killed our people and we fought back. Then Father tells of a wounded American running from the Japanese. Our tribe hid him, but he died a few days later."

Joe was suddenly excited.

"Did he have a vial?" he asked, his eyes alert. He knew it was a long shot, but the idea that they might still be able to save their father put his nerves instantly on edge.

When Bidai translated, the Ukit's eyes narrowed. He looked as if he were trying to see inside the boys' minds to judge their intentions. Finally he nodded.

"Do you still have it?" Frank asked quickly.

"Yes," Isat said, motioning for the others to follow him. "My father has shown it to me," Bidai translated.

He started through the trees slowly at first, then faster as he saw that Joe and Frank could keep up. Bidai brought up the rear, watching for Assassins. As Joe and Frank had guessed, now that they had the map, the Assassins were no longer interested in the Hardys.

Isat stopped in front of a low cave in an outcropping of rock. He signaled for the others to wait, said a few words to Bidai, and disappeared inside.

"Isat's tribe still lives like the Ukits of a hundred years ago, traveling through the jungle, killing game with their blowpipes for food. They sometimes harvest camphor to trade for knives and other tools. They do not build permanent houses but keep their most precious belongings in hiding places. This must be one of them."

As he finished speaking, Isat returned holding a fat clay pot the size of a cantaloupe. The top was plugged with bark. Isat removed the bark and withdrew a large carved nutshell from the pot. It had been cut in half so that one half was a small bowl and the other was the lid. It was sealed with pitch that had become brittle with age. Isat used his knife to chip away the seal and lifted the lid carefully. Inside, on a bed of dried grass, lay a small glass vial still capped with a plug and labeled in Japanese. The liquid it held was pale green.

"I'll tell my father I gave it to the Americans," Isat said through Bidai, handing it to Frank reverently. "Just like the wounded soldier said."

Frank smiled back and tried to thank Isat graciously, but his heart raced as his hands closed around the nutshell case holding the medicine he desperately needed to cure his father. Now all they had to do was get back to the hospital.

"But we lost the boat," Joe gasped. "It'll take days to walk out of the jungle."

Isat frowned when Bidai explained.

"There's a canoe by the river," Isat replied. "We keep it for going to town but don't use it much. I'll show you."

Isat took off for the river, picking out narrow game trails that made the going easy. Within an hour they were standing just below the rapids where their own canoe had been washed away.

Isat jogged back into the jungle several feet from the river and parted the branches of a thorn bush. Inside was a dugout canoe similar to the one they had come up the river in, but with no motor.

With Joe and Bidai on one side and Frank and Isat on the other, they got the canoe to the water quickly and climbed in. Joe and Bidai grabbed the two oars in the bottom of the boat.

Just before they pushed off, Frank turned to Isat. "I'll never forget you," he said respectfully. "If our father lives, it will be because of you." He held out his hand, and Isat shook it firmly.

Then Frank turned and helped Joe and Bidai push off from shore into the main current that would carry them back down the river to Kijang. When Frank glanced back, Isat was gone.

The rain-swollen channel was running madly, promising a perilous ride. The trip downriver would be faster than the ascent, but it would also be far more dangerous.

They battled the water for three hours, dodging rocks and logs. Joe's muscles ached. "The next rapids look bad," he said as he and Bidai paddled the canoe down a calm stretch of river.

Bidai nodded. Up ahead, the river dove down a steep rapids a hundred yards long, lashing around a huge boulder in the middle of the channel.

"We'll stay to the right," Bidai yelled as they

approached the boulder. But even as he spoke, Frank saw a pair of large logs jammed among the rocks on their right.

"No, it's blocked," he cried.

"Left then," Bidai called, and he and Joe switched their paddles to the opposite side of the canoe. They paddled furiously, barely making it to the left of the huge rock, then had to face the worst of the rapids.

"Hang on to that vial!" Joe yelled as the canoe headed straight for another rock.

Frank clutched the side of the canoe with one hand, the hollowed-out nut with the other. They were coming closer to a jagged rock that jutted out of the swirling white water, and Joe and Bidai's paddling couldn't push them clear.

"I'll try," Frank yelled back. Just then the front of the canoe crashed into the boulder and shot skyward as it slid over the top. The canoe pitched wildly. Joe was thrown into the water, and Bidai was tossed into the bottom of the boat.

Frank's impulse was to drop the nutshell and grab onto the side with both hands, but if he did, all hope of saving their father would be washed overboard. He gritted his teeth and clenched the side of the canoe with his left hand.

The bow of the boat slid off the side of the boulder and back into the water. Bidai and Frank leaned hard to the right and managed to keep the canoe from flipping over. Then Bidai pulled himself back to his seat to maneuver the rest of the rapids. Joe caught the back of the canoe and held on until they reached calmer water, then climbed back in.

Frank gave a heavy sigh. "Let's not do that again," he said, peeking inside the shell. The vial was unharmed.

"We won't have to," Bidai said, pointing down the river. "There's my longhouse."

Within minutes they had pulled the canoe up to the dock and were racing toward Bidai's car. They leaped over the doors and were on their way to the hospital before the Iban children even had a chance to gather at the river to welcome them back. Rain had turned the dusty ruts of the road into a bog, forcing Bidai to drive slowly. When they finally reached the hospital, Joe's muscles were tense from anticipation.

"Watch out for Medicine Man," Frank whispered as they half walked, half jogged down the hall of the Kijang hospital.

"Yeah, whoever that is," Joe muttered. He pushed open the door to Fenton's room, and Al sprang to his feet, then relaxed when he saw who was there. Dr. Tokunaga was on the opposite side of Fenton's bed and seemed startled by their entrance. Thomas Wilson was next to her.

Fenton was breathing rapidly, and Frank and Joe immediately spotted the straps holding his arms to the sides of the bed. That had to mean the convulsions had started. Fenton was in the final stages of anthrax-B.

"We've got the cure," Joe said. Opening the shell, he lifted out the vial. "Give this to him now, it's his only chance."

"What is it?" Dr. Tokunaga asked, eyeing the vial suspiciously.

"I don't know," Joe said impatiently. "Just give it to him. I'll take responsibility."

"I'm not going to administer some strange concoction without knowing what it is," Dr. Tokunaga said.

"Let me," Thomas volunteered. His voice was calm and friendly, and he quickly stepped toward Joe, his hand outstretched.

For a moment Joe thought his problem was solved. Thomas could administer the cure just as well as Dr. Tokunaga. Something made Joe uneasy and he hesitated. Thomas's expression became angry.

"Give it to me now," Thomas demanded, stepping closer to Joe.

"No!" Joe said trying to yank his hand back. It was too late. Thomas's left hand wrapped around Joe's wrist. Joe ducked and just managed to dodge a blow from Thomas's right fist.

Frank and Bidai jumped quickly to Joe's aid. Seeing he was outnumbered, Thomas made one last attempt to get the vial by slamming Joe's hand against the wall.

Joe didn't let go, but as the back of his hand crashed against the wood, he felt the vial shatter inside his fist.

Chapter

16

"No! DON'T LET IT BREAK!" Frank yelled as he leaped to tear Thomas off his brother. It was too late.

Joe felt a splinter of broken glass stab into his palm. The precious liquid leaked out through his fingers and onto the floor. The cure was gone.

Frank and Al threw Thomas onto the floor.

Joe sank back against the wall and leaned there for support, opening his hand to look at the crushed vial. As he pulled a sliver of glass from his palm, the door to Fenton's room opened again.

"How's he feel?"

It was the Gray Man, and as he surveyed the room, his forehead creased into a frown.

"We had the cure," Joe said in disbelief. "We

found the vial from the Japanese lab, but Thomas broke it."

"You should have let me have it," Thomas growled as he struggled to his feet between Frank and Al.

"You're Medicine Man, aren't you?" Frank said, wrenching Thomas's arm behind his back.

"Yes," Thomas said, wincing. "And I should have made sure you were finished off in the jungle."

"Then you were the one who heard Dad say he'd sent the map to us," Joe said. "And you sent those thugs after us."

"That's right," Thomas said with a sneer. "And now nobody gets the cure, including your dad."

The Gray Man motioned for Garribay to hold Thomas, then stepped to Joe's side and began examining the pieces of the crushed vial that still lay in his palm. The Gray Man picked up the label with shards of glass still clinging to it and carefully straightened it out.

"It was from the leaf of a plant," Gray Man said after a moment. "It probably wouldn't have worked after fifty years anyway."

"What kind of plant?" Joe asked, excited.

"I can't tell exactly," the Gray Man said, shaking his head. "Plants aren't my specialty, but from this, I'd guess it's in the orchid family."

"There are hundreds of orchids in Borneo," Dr. Tokunaga said sadly. "Let me see."

Dr. Tokunaga took the label from the Gray

Man and studied the words. "It *is* a member of the orchid family," she announced. "It grows in Borneo, but it's unusual. We could never find one in time to save your father. It has purple flowers and a strong scent of vanilla."

Frank and Joe looked at each other and then at Bidai.

"Jungle Mulvaney's!" Joe shouted, pushing past the Gray Man toward the door. "There's a vine there that smells like vanilla."

"And has purple flowers," Frank added, following Joe out the door.

Bidai was right behind them as they raced to the car and jumped in. He drove as fast as he could, powering through mud bogs toward Jungle Mulvaney's tree house.

They ran along the path and, after a quick explanation to Jungle, took several stems from the vine, making sure there were plenty of green leaves.

"Thanks," Joe yelled to Jungle Mulvaney as they swung to the ground under the tree house.

"I hope it works," Mulvaney yelled after them.

"Me, too," Joe murmured and caught Frank's hand in a high five as they headed back down the path.

"I have to warn you, this is a long shot," Dr. Tokunaga said as she stood ready to give Fenton a brew she'd steeped from the leaves.

It was dark outside. Joe and Frank had

watched the sun set as Bidai drove recklessly back to the hospital. It had been exactly seven days since Fenton arrived at the hospital sick. If the tonic didn't work, he would be dead by morning.

"We're used to long shots," Joe said, pacing nervously outside the plastic tent that still covered Fenton's bed.

Fenton's breathing sounded like panting now, and the convulsions were coming more frequently.

Joe and Frank swallowed hard as Dr. Tokunaga put some of the liquid into the intravenous tube that had been used to give Fenton food and water since he lost consciousness.

When she finished, she stepped back from the bed, closed the plastic curtains, and pulled off her surgical mask.

"Now we wait," she said.

Joe and Frank stood beside their father's bed until late in the night. Neither of them could stand to sit while they waited to see if their father would live. Once each hour Dr. Tokunaga came in, listened to Fenton's heart, took his pulse, and shook her head. At 3:00 A.M. there was still no change. Exhausted from their own ordeal, Frank and Joe slumped into chairs and dozed.

"How do you get a drink in this place?"

The hoarse voice brought Joe slowly out of his fitful sleep. The voice sounded familiar, but it took him a minute to recognize it as his father's. "Doctor!" he yelled, finally coming fully awake. He ran to Fenton's bed. Frank was beside him.

Fenton peered up through the plastic tent and smiled.

Frank turned to the door and yelled into the hall, "Doctor! He's awake."

Dr. Tokunaga was at Fenton's bedside within minutes. She felt his forehead, took his pulse, and finally smiled.

"It worked," she announced, and quickly helped Fenton drink some water from a cup.

"You look tired," Fenton said to his sons. They both laughed.

"You don't look so great yourself," Frank said, helping Joe pull the plastic tent away from the bed. They were no longer afraid of catching anthrax-B. "How do you feel?"

"Beat," Fenton answered. "But something tells me I'm lucky to be here at all."

"You are," Dr. Tokunaga said. "And you have your sons to thank."

"I'm not surprised," Fenton said, smiling. "What have I missed?"

"A lot," Joe said as he and Frank cranked up their father's bed.

"But you'll have plenty of time to talk about it," said a voice from behind them.

They turned to see the Gray Man standing at the door. "The Network lab is testing an extract from the leaves," he said, his arms folded. "Initial findings show it kills anthrax-B bacteria on contact, and Fenton is living proof."

"You found the cure for anthrax-B?" Fenton asked.

"Joe and Frank found it," the Gray Man said. "Unfortunately, it doesn't seem to work on common anthrax, so it wasn't the cure Phillips Pharmaceuticals was hoping for. Finding it does foil the Assassins, though. They have no way to blackmail anyone with the mutant strain now."

"How do you know about Phillips Pharmaceuticals?" Fenton asked the Gray Man.

"We've been watching everyone who was looking for the cure," the Gray Man said.

"What about Thomas?" Frank asked.

Dr. Tokunaga's eyes suddenly locked onto the Gray Man as she, too, waited for the answer.

"Thomas pinpointed the Assassins' lab in Pakistan," the Gray Man said. "He ordered the ransacking of Fenton's office in Bayport, as well as the attack and blackmailing attempt on you here in Borneo."

The Gray Man frowned at Dr. Tokunaga. "He also murdered your lab assistant so he could take over the job. The Assassins have been looking for the cure here in Borneo for weeks, and Thomas figured this job would be a good cover while he supervised the operation. He sneaked through the window in the lab and injected your assistant with curare poison so his death would look like the result of a heart attack. It was an Assassin operative Dr. Tokunaga walked in on in the lab a few days ago, too. Apparently he had come for a meeting with Thomas. When he was discovered, he used the Iban shield to mask his identity."

"And it was probably Thomas who planted the rupees on Dr. Tokunaga's desk," Frank said.

The doctor's expression grew steely. "So Thomas is a murderer. But did he cause Mr. Hardy's illness, too?"

"Apparently, yes, though we're not sure how or why," the Gray Man said.

"I came to the hospital for records about anthrax-B," Fenton said at last. "The doctor wasn't here, so I talked to Thomas. I didn't know until later what a mistake that was. I had the map by then, and Thomas seemed like a helpful guy, so I asked him to recommend a guide to take me into the jungle. He said he knew someone, and they'd be in touch. That night at the White Hornbill, I was visited by some thugs who held me at knife point and went through my luggage."

"They must have been looking for the map," Frank said, still standing close to his father's bed.

"That's right. They even asked me about it when they couldn't find it themselves," Fenton went on. "Of course, I didn't tell them it was in the secret compartment of my suitcase the whole time. Anyway, one of them jammed a dart into my neck and told me they'd be back when I was ready to talk."

"When did you know the dart had infected you with anthrax-B?" Joe asked with interest.

"I was sick by morning," Fenton said. "I barely made it to the airport and begged an English tourist to take the map back to London with him. He promised to drop it off at an overnight courier service there. Then I staggered up to the hospital, where Thomas offered to share the cure if I handed over the map. That's when I knew for sure he was the one who sent the thugs to my room. I passed out pretty soon after that."

"So when you woke up and said, 'Get the doctor. He's the one,' you didn't mean Dr. Tokunaga at all."

Fenton looked puzzled. "I do remember waking up just long enough to see you, and I vaguely remember trying to warn you. Then everything went black again," Fenton said. "It makes sense I'd call for Dr. Tokunaga—even though I don't know why I referred to her as a *he*. *She* worked hard to save me from the beginning, and I trusted her, even if she doesn't ever smile."

Dr. Tokunaga's face turned red, and at first Frank and Joe thought she was getting angry again. Then she threw her hands up in despair and sank into one of the chairs.

"My grandfather was in Borneo in World War Two," she said. "I know there are horror stories about things Japanese soldiers did here, but

Grandfather liked this place, and when I heard his stories, I knew Borneo was where I wanted to work as a doctor. I came here to help people. But they've never accepted me—maybe because I'm Japanese. That's why I wanted to keep the anthrax-B a secret. I figured if people knew there was a Japanese biological weapon loose, they would blame me."

Frank suddenly felt a pang of guilt about suspecting the doctor of being an Assassin. He decided to talk to Bidai about her. Maybe the headman's son could convince the other Ibans to be more friendly.

"What about the Ibans? Were any of them involved with the Assassins?" Frank asked. "Some of the men who attacked us looked like they could have been Ibans."

The Gray Man shook his head. "No, but I wouldn't be surprised if the Assassins disguised themselves as Ibans so that anyone who got a look at them would blame the locals."

"I can't believe we were taken in by Thomas," Joe said. "By the time we got here, he knew we had the map. No wonder he was so nice to us."

"Yeah, and all the time he was just egging us on. He wanted us to find out that Dad had anthrax-B so we'd head out into the jungle and the Assassins could follow. And we bought the whole act," Frank said. "We even told him where we were going."

"Don't feel too bad," Fenton said, frowning.

"If I hadn't fallen for his act, maybe none of this would have happened."

"At least we found the cure in time," Frank said, smiling.

"Yeah," Joe agreed. "But just barely."

Two days later Dr. Tokunaga declared Fenton well enough to travel. They packed their bags and checked out of the White Hornbill. Bidai took them to the hospital to get Fenton and, after thanking Dr. Tokunaga, they all crowded into Bidai's little green car and headed for the airport.

As they waited for the small plane, Frank pulled a small package from his bag.

"It's an early birthday present," he said to Bidai. "From all of us."

Bidai opened the brown paper wrapper carefully and let out a long "Wow!" when he saw the contents—a large box of alkaline batteries and a new game cartridge for his video game. Laura Hardy had sent them over by Crazy Jay's courier service.

"It's a good gift," Bidai said, smiling. "And maybe things will calm down enough for me to play, once you Hardys are gone." Then he reached under his bulky shirt and took two belts from his waist and handed one to each of the guys.

Joe recognized the rich brown, black, and tan markings on the leather. It was from the skin of the python they had killed in the jungle.

"I made them myself," Bidai said with pride.

Frank felt a lump in his throat as the loudspeaker blared out the last call for their flight. He shook Bidai's hand firmly. When he was done, Joe did the same.

"You can come and visit us in Bayport anytime," Joe said. "We don't do much python wrestling there, but you'd probably play a great game of football."

Frank and Joe's next case:

Ron Minkus was one of the hottest radio personalities around. His specialty: being a totally obnoxious, equal opportunity offender who'd make nasty jokes about anyone, anytime. In other words, he made a living making enemies. But he's not making a living anymore. The electrifying personality has been electrocuted! The Hardys' investigation leads them to a gang of skinhead thugs known as the Bootstompers. The gang has had run-ins with Minkus before, and for Frank and Joe it quickly turns into a running battle of fists, fireballs, and firebombs. But the real trouble is only beginning—the boys are closing in on a killer with a cold heart and a deadly plan ... in *Shock Jock,* Case #106 in The Hardy Boys Casefiles™.

THE HARDY BOYS CASEFILES™
